T5-BQB-612

Dear Romance Reader,

Welcome to a world of breathtaking passion and never-ending romance.

Welcome to *Precious Gem Romances*.

It is our pleasure to present *Precious Gem Romances*, a wonderful new line of romance books by some of America's best-loved authors. Let these thrilling historical and contemporary romances sweep you away to far-off times and places in stories that will dazzle your senses and melt your heart.

Sparkling with joy, laughter, and love, each *Precious Gem Romance* glows with all the passion and excitement you expect from the very best in romance. Offered at a great affordable price, these books are an irresistible value—and an essential addition to your romance collection. Tender love stories you will want to read again and again, *Precious Gem Romances* are books you will treasure forever.

Look for eight fabulous new *Precious Gem Romances* each month—available only at Wal★Mart.

Lynn Brown, Publisher

FIRST LOVE, LAST LOVE

Victoria Chancellor

Zebra Books
Kensington Publishing Corp.

http://www.zebrabooks.com

*To Martha "Bun" Garrett and Dorothy Semones, two
wonderful sisters who aren't the least bit interfering!
Thanks for your encouragement and support all these years,
and for making me a part of your family.*

ZEBRA BOOKS are published by

Kensington Publishing Corp.
850 Third Avenue
New York, NY 10022

Zebra and the Z logo Reg. U.S. Pat. & TM Off.

First Printing: December, 1997
10 9 8 7 6 5 4 3 2 1

Printed in the United States of America

Chapter One

"And now, a very generous, warm, and loving donation from our resident pet expert and owner of Pet's Plus, Jillian Snow."

Jillian smiled at her friend Brenda, then looked out over the audience that filled the theater. Recognition and a smattering of applause were unnecessary. These people were her friends and neighbors. They knew she always donated something from her pet store for the Valentine's Day benefit. This year, she'd decided to match up a kitten or puppy with a loving family. After all, everyone—every*thing*—deserved love on Valentine's Day.

So why was she spending the evening at a community benefit instead of snuggling up to some handsome devil on her sofa? *Because you're just too darn picky,* she answered her own question, stepping forward, smiling, and giving the audience a small wave to get this show on the road. *And maybe because you've never met another man who curls your toes like the one who broke your heart,* she silently added.

"Let's start the bidding for a puppy or kitten, food and goodies, at twenty-five dollars," Brenda continued when the audience settled back down to the serious business of the annual Valentine's Day auction. "And remember that Jillian will give personal attention to whoever is the highest bidder, making sure your new pet is settled into your home."

Brenda should be on one of the home shopping channels, Jillian thought, amused at her friend's various skills.

"Twenty-five dollars from Mrs. Crabtree. Do I hear thirty? Thirty from Dr. Taylor at the Women's Clinic. Thirty-five from our new librarian, Mandy Thompson."

Brenda knew everyone in town, Jillian thought with a smile. Gossip was Brenda's full-time job now that her daughter was in school. Before that momentous event, she'd had to juggle child care with obtaining and passing along "special news" about her friends and neighbors.

Jillian kept the smile on her face as she looked up the aisle toward the darker rows of the small, old theater. She'd come here nearly every weekend when she was a child, and the smells of popcorn and spilled soda were still the same. She and Brenda and sometimes Brad, Brenda's twin, race-walking, giggling, jostling down the aisles, trying to get the best seats without making so much noise that they'd get a stern lecture from Mr. Potter. Or, even worse, that he'd tell their parents the next time they ran into each other at the grocery store or church. You just couldn't get away with much around Mr. Potter.

Now, when she occasionally went to a movie in the Scottsville theater rather than the larger complex in Tyler, she was thankful he still ran it with a firm—albeit more aged and wrinkled—hand and a sharp ear for kids who disrupted the show.

Boy, was she getting old! It seemed like just yesterday when she and Brenda sat side-by-side, with Brad two or three rows back, throwing Gummy Bears at them. The silly memory made her smile again.

She could almost imagine the little boy who was skipping down the row as her childhood tormentor, except this boy was too young, and his hand was firmly held by a striking figure of a man. Too bad the darkness kept her from seeing who approached. He looked vaguely familiar, she thought as he raised his hand in greeting to someone on the stage, but she couldn't place him. Not that Scottsville had many newcomers. She'd just like to know. Darn, she was getting as nosy as—

"And fifty dollars from my dear brother Brad Patterson, who has just moved back to Scottsville!"

A smattering of applause punctuated the elevator drop that

was her stomach. Jillian felt her mouth fall open like a dead guppy. She probably resembled one too, with her eyes round and her skin pasty white. At least, that's how she felt. Brad Patterson was moving back to town? Why hadn't someone told her? Why hadn't *Brenda* told her?

She tore her gaze away from the man now standing in the light from the stage—the man with broad shoulders and slim hips, holding the hand of a boy that had to be his son Jeremy— and stared a hole through Brenda. Unfortunately, her friend went on happily taking bids, pushing up the price to sixty-five dollars with a smile and a bit of chatter about everyone.

Darn it, Brenda, why didn't you tell me? Jillian wanted to ask. Why surprise me in front of practically the whole town? She felt like running for the curtains, down the back stairs and out into the early darkness and cool temperatures of this February night. She was sure her cheeks, at least, had gone from pasty white to fluorescent pink.

"Seventy-five," her childhood nemesis announced in a clear, deep voice. Jillian's attention snapped back to the later arrivals. Jeremy jumped up and down beside his dad, clearly delighted with the bidding. Darn it, this wasn't fair! When had Brad's voice gotten so rich and soft? When had he gone from gangly teenager to hunky father?

She narrowed her eyes. While he was off at Texas A & M, making new friends, dating other girls. Marrying someone else. Yeah, that's when, she reminded herself, staring a hole through him now. However, he was just as oblivious to her darkening thoughts as his twin sister, who was trying to drive up the price even higher.

One other bid came in from the doctor, then Brad spoke up again. "Let's make it an even hundred," he said with a charming smile that had everyone agog. Jeremy tugged on his hand, trying to pull him closer to the stage.

No, no, no! Jillian wanted to shout the words. She didn't want to deal with Brad, helping *him* pick out a puppy or a kitten for another woman's child. Showing *him* how to feed the little critter, litter box or paper train it, and give it toys for teething and amusement. This wasn't fair!

"Going once, going twice," Brenda said in a cheerful voice,

looking around the theater. "Sold to Brad and Jeremy Patterson for one hundred dollars."

Jillian watched as father and son approached. Brad looked at her with intense, all-knowing eyes that seemed slightly amused by the whole scenario. His lips turned up ever so slightly in what she preferred to think of as a smirk. Certainly not a real smile. The man could have purchased a pet for his son anywhere else for far less than a hundred dollars. No, he'd bid on purpose, to make her uncomfortable. He might as well be throwing gummy bears at her again!

The urge to run was stronger the closer he got, but she wasn't about to show him how much she wanted to be anywhere but on this stage. As he swung Jeremy up the steps onto the old wooden floor, Jillian suppressed her need to jump back. Brad took the steps two at a time, still smiling—or smirking, depending on one's attitude—while he approached his sister.

Brenda immediately rushed to Jillian's side, giving her a bone-crushing hug and a big dramatic smile. The move made Brad alter his approach, turning toward her now. She swallowed the feeling of panic that threatened to overwhelm all her senses.

"Why didn't you tell me?" she whispered to Brenda between clenched teeth.

Brenda simply raised her eyebrows in an innocent look that wouldn't have fooled anyone. "Isn't this the best?" she gushed to everyone within earshot. "The three of us, just like in the old days!"

"Hardly," Jillian whispered, again for Brenda's ears only. Humiliating oneself wasn't the goal of the Valentine's Day benefit, although the Patterson twins seemed to be intent on that very goal.

"Jilly," Brad said in that deep, bedroom voice that he'd acquired sometime in the last eleven years.

"It's Jillian," she said, raising her chin. "Or, if you prefer, Miss Snow."

Brad gave her a dark, soul searching look for just a moment before his nostrils flared and his lips twitched. No doubt in amusement, Jillian thought. Then he bent toward his son.

"Jeremy, this is Miss Snow. She owns the pet store where we're going to get your new puppy."

"Yeah!"

"Jeremy . . ." Brad said in warning.

"Sorry," the cute little boy said in a non-apologetic voice before rushing on. "Hello, Miss Snow. When can I come and get my puppy?"

"Hello, Jeremy. You can come by anytime the store's open. Maybe your aunt Brenda would like to bring you over? I'd sure like to talk to her," Jillian said, ignoring Brad and giving his sister what she hoped was a look that would chill red pepper sauce.

"Oh, I just couldn't," Brenda said, sidling away from Jillian. "I have so much to do for the benefit. Doing a final tabulation, calling people. I'm sure you understand. Now I have to get busy with the auction. You two get acquainted again," Brenda said with a big smile.

"She should be wearing a T-shirt that says 'matchmaker,'" Jillian murmured.

"Pardon me?" Brad said. "I didn't catch that."

"You weren't supposed to," Jillian replied, not looking at him. "So, Jeremy, you'd like a puppy rather than a kitten?"

"Yeah! A really cool puppy. Do you have any of the spotted ones like in the movie?"

"What movie?"

"The Disney movie from a couple of years ago. It's his favorite video," Brad explained. "He means Dalmatians."

"Yeah, Dalmatians! I want one of those."

"I'm sorry, but I don't have any Dalmatians, Jeremy. Maybe you and your father would like to wait until I get some in."

"And when would that be?" Brad asked in an amused voice, as though he knew exactly what she was thinking.

"Oh, who knows? I'm sure eventually someone in the area will get a Dalmatian and have some puppies."

"Could be years."

Jillian shrugged "Could be."

"I think we'll go with what you have in stock."

"I wouldn't want to rush you," she replied. "Jeremy might have his heart set on a Dalmatian."

"I'm sure he can find something else he'll like just as much."

"I don't know—"

"Daddy, I want a puppy," Jeremy said, trying to interrupt.

"I believe I know both you *and* my son pretty well," Brad

said in an amused voice that compelled her to look at him once again. He ignored his son's comment, focusing totally on Jillian. The heat from the stage lights sent a whiff of his cologne toward her, making her draw in a deep breath as she tried to discount his looks.

"I figure you'll get in a Dalmatian puppy about the time he goes off to college," he tossed out lightly.

Jillian noticed a few of her fellow shopkeepers walk up behind Brad on the theater floor, ready to talk. Well, she wasn't about to let him go. Not with that juicy line dangling in front of her.

"Oh, would that be before or after he broke up with his childhood sweetheart?" Jillian said with enough sarcasm to stop him in his tracks.

"Daddy—"

"Score one for the angry pet store owner," Brad said, losing some of his amusement as he made an imaginary mark with his right forefinger.

"Who's angry?" Millicent Gardner asked, her lavender-gray curls tipped to one side as she peered up onto the stage. "This is supposed to be fun."

"Yes, isn't it," Jillian replied, crossing her arms over her chest. "I haven't had this much fun in eleven years."

"Oh, my," Millicent's sister Greta said. "I think we've come at a bad time."

"Not at all," Brad said, turning to the ladies. He hunkered down on the stage so the elderly women wouldn't have to look up so far.

Oh, yes, ever the thoughtful one, Jillian thought. So thoughtful that he'd purchased a puppy from the one person who never wanted to see him again. Who couldn't stand the sight of him. Who didn't want to be in the same theater with him!

Mr. Potter walked up, joining the ladies. "Well, well. Brad Patterson. Haven't seen you in ages."

"I've got to go," Jillian announced, unwilling to participate in the Patterson fan club. "Some of us have to work tomorrow."

"We're working tomorrow," Millicent supplied, obviously a bit confused by the hostility lurking just beneath polite conversation.

"Of course you are. We couldn't get through the morning

without a fresh cinnamon roll and coffee from the Gardner Bakery,'' Jillian said with a smile for the two older women.

"She means him," Greta whispered to Millicent, giving her sister a little punch in the ribs.

"As a matter of fact, I'm working tomorrow too," Brad said. "I may even bring my computer down to the bakery and work there for a couple of hours."

"Oh, my. We've never had a computer in the bakery before."

"I'm sure you'll survive," Jillian said as she walked down the steps. "It probably doesn't eat much."

Mr. Potter laughed. Jeremy giggled. "I'll see you tomorrow, Jeremy, if your dad can pull himself away from the cyber-cafe long enough." She channel-surfed cable television enough to throw around a high-tech phrase or two!

She couldn't resist watching Brad's blue-gray eyes narrow. They no longer appeared so warm and inviting. Good. She didn't want warmth, teasing, or anything else from Brad Patterson. She didn't even want him in her town.

"I'm sure I can find time," he replied. "As a matter of fact, we may need lots of time for Jeremy to make up his mind. Hours, even. And then there's all that personal attention you promised."

Hours with Brad and his son in her small shop, or giving him "personal attention" wherever he'd be living? She didn't think so. If necessary, she'd paint black spots on a white puppy and pass it off as a genuine Dalmatian—a direct descendent of one of those movie dogs—before she'd allow him to linger any longer than necessary.

"I'm usually pretty busy. Let's try to make it brief."

"That's not a very charitable attitude, Jilly."

"I reserve my charity for valid organizations, not for every man who happens to drift through town. And that's Miss Snow to you. As in cold, pristine, untouchable *snow*."

"Or one might say harsh and frigid snow," Brad replied, his own eyes narrowed.

Jillian place both fists on her hips. "One might, if one wanted a black eye."

"Daddy, does it snow here much? It don't snow much in Houston."

"Not now, Jeremy." Brad advanced toward the stairs. "Or as in Snow White?"

The old nickname nearly pushed her over the edge. Her nails bit into her clenched fists as her childhood nemesis walked closer. "That's enough."

He stopped well within her personal space, making her want to step back. She didn't, although she wished she had when she inhaled deeply and smelled the rich scent of his cologne . . . again.

"Or how about pure, melt in your mouth snow," he whispered. "I remember eating snow just like that one time. Very fresh, very tasty."

Her face heated so fast she felt as though she might go up in flames. How dare he? The urge to smack that all-knowing look off his face was so strong that only years of overcoming the stigma of a redhead's temper kept her hands clenched at her sides.

"Not very filling, though, was it?" she said through clenched teeth. "One minute it's snow, and the next it's just plain old melted water."

She turned on her heel before he could say anything else, nearly running up the aisle to escape his presence. Oh, Lord, why had he decided to move back to town? This couldn't be happening to her. Not now . . . not again. Life wasn't fair!

The darkness of the February night surrounded her as she pushed open the double glass doors and rushed from the theater onto the town square. The cool air caressed her warm cheeks. And what was that moisture—rain? No, not a cloud in the sky. She dashed away the tears with a swipe of her hand as she headed for her apartment above the pet store.

Darn it, this town just wasn't big enough for both of them! And as far as she was concerned, Brad had given up any right to call Scottsville home eleven years ago when he'd driven off to college . . . and out of her life.

Brad shut the door to Jeremy's bedroom, listened for a moment to make sure the tired but active four year old didn't try to get out of bed for a last few minutes of play before succumbing to sleep. All was quiet in the big old house. Just a few creaky floorboards, he noticed as he tread lightly toward the stairs. He'd have to get them fixed . . . or maybe he'd leave the squeak so that Jeremy couldn't sneak out of the house when he became a teenager. Looking at his son now, that time seemed far away. But Brad knew how fast time could fly. Just look at how quickly eleven years had passed. Eleven years since he'd moved away from Scottsville and out of Jillian's life, he mused as he walked slowly downstairs.

Lord, how she'd changed! He'd only seen her from a distance when he'd returned briefly to visit Brenda and her family. Unknown to his former girlfriend, he'd drive by her pet store, or cruise by her father's house just on the outskirts of town. Once he'd seen Jillian working in the yard; another time he'd seen her through the window of the store, laughing with a customer. But he hadn't seen her up close and personal. His gut still hurt from the figurative punch he'd taken when he'd seen her standing on the stage, wearing a form-fitting red dress, smiling out at the audience.

He flicked on the overhead light in the kitchen and headed toward the refrigerator. The curly, carrot-top hair that had given Jilly such fits as a child had turned into shimmering waves of red and gold. Her freckles had been tamed, but he noticed a few scattered across her nose and perched on her high cheek-bones. Her skin was still pale and clear, as unlined and fresh as when she was seventeen.

And that tall, gangly girl's body had filled out in all the right places—even more so than when he'd explored it as thoroughly as possible in stolen moments beside the lake, in his car, and on her couch when her parents played cards. The memory of her pale, freckled breasts and firm, round bottom caused a reaction that any teenage boy—not to mention a twenty-nine-year-old man—would have been proud of.

He grabbed a cold soda from the fridge and thought briefly of using it to cool off the memory-induced reaction. Shaking his head and laughing at his plight, he settled his hips against the counter and popped the lid. Did Jillian have any idea what she was doing to him right now? Probably not. She no doubt assumed he was angry over her caustic remarks. Well, he had been, but not for long. He couldn't hold a grudge when what he really wanted was to kiss the bitterness from her lips. Not when his goal was to make her remember the good times and believe that there were many more ahead.

Moving back to Scottsville hadn't been entirely for Jeremy, as Brad had told Brenda and anyone else who'd asked. He might have moved to any small town where children could still play in front yards and walk downtown safely. Brad knew he could have relocated somewhere else with good schools and a strong sense of community. Maybe even somewhere closer to Houston, where his ex-wife still lived and worked.

But Jillian didn't live in *those* small towns. After four years of college and several years of marriage to a woman so unlike his former sweetheart that they could barely be compared, he'd returned to his senses. He'd returned to Jillian.

Of course, she didn't know that yet . . . and he wasn't about to tell her the real reason he was back in Scottsville. Not that she'd believe him, he thought as he took a sip from the sweating can. Her cutting remarks about their break-up and his purchase of a pet for Jeremy had hurt, plus they'd reminded him what an uphill battle winning her back was going to be. He was up for the challenge, though. He had an arsenal full of weapons, not the least of which was their still smoldering desire for one another.

Oh, she'd tried to hide it, he knew. But he'd seen the look of interest on her face before she'd realized who was walking down the aisle toward her. He'd seen the way she protected herself by hugging her arms across her breasts. She'd fisted her hands to keep from popping him a good one. She'd looked into his eyes, reacting with a woman's instinct when she noticed the interest there. Oh yes, Jillian wanted him, too. She just wouldn't admit it to herself yet.

Soon, he swore as he finished the can of soda. He crushed the aluminum in one hand, then scored a three-pointer in the trash can across the room. Soon, he vowed, smiling to himself as he flipped off the light and walked toward his bedroom.

Chapter Two

"You didn't call me back last night."

"I wasn't sure you'd still be up when I got in. The benefit was—"

Jillian shifted the phone to her shoulder as she scooped hamster food into the cage. "You thought I might just go home early and go to sleep after you and your brother drop a bombshell on me? Did I miss the medical report that I've gone into a coma?"

"Now, Jillian—"

"Don't 'now, Jillian' me, you traitor. Why didn't you tell me he was moving back to town?"

"You didn't like the surprise?" Brenda asked tentatively.

Jillian snorted into the phone. "As if you thought I would."

"Well, I thought you might," Brenda said in a weak, small voice that she usually reserved for explaining some "absolutely essential" purchases to her husband.

"I really don't need this," Jillian said, narrowing her eyes at the nervous little critters who chased each other through their tunnels and around their food dishes.

"You and Brad were so close once."

"That was more than eleven years ago, Brenda, and we didn't exactly part on the best of terms."

"All the more reason to see each other again, to put the past behind you."

"The past was behind me until *he* showed up."

Jillian heard Brenda's sigh. "Are you really mad at me?"

"Furious." Jillian placed the lid on the hamster's cage and moved on to the two guinea pigs that she'd just gotten in. The long-haired furballs were more calm than the hamsters, but they were still getting used to their new home.

New home. Hmm . . .

"Where's he living, Brenda? And how did he buy a house in Scottsville without everyone knowing about it?"

"He bought that big Victorian house with the turret room on the side."

"The one on Spindletop Street?"

"That's the one."

"So why didn't I hear about it? What did he do to keep the sale a secret?"

"He bought it under his company's name. He's going to be working out of the house as well as living there."

"Great," Jillian said, frowning at the image of Brad just a few streets away. "Sounds like he's really moved in."

"You really don't seem excited," Brenda said, her voice revealing her disappointment.

"Of course I'm not excited—unless you think furious means the same thing. I can't imagine why you'd think this would be a good surprise."

"Well, I had hoped—"

"Don't start hoping for anything, Brenda. Do you hear me?" Jillian asked, punctuating her sentences with waves of the food scoop. "Absolutely nothing is going to happen between Brad and me."

"You could at least sit down and talk."

"I don't need to talk to him. Look, Brenda, I know he's your brother and you think he's a great guy, but *he's* the one who ended our engagement. *He's* the one who needed freedom to date other girls, to make other friends. I didn't run off and start a new life in Houston."

"That's just where he got his first job. That's not where his heart is."

"I don't know where his heart is, and furthermore, I don't care." Jillian stabbed the food scoop into the bin and closed the lid with a resounding thunk.

"Then you don't think you and Brad can go back to being friends."

She closed her eyes against the pain that pounded against her temples. Whether it was from the conversation or memories, she couldn't tell. The source really didn't matter. All that mattered was that she stay away from Brad Patterson. She wasn't interested in why he'd moved back to town, what he'd been doing the last eleven years, or what he was going to do with the rest of his life.

"No, Brenda, I don't think we'll ever be friends again," Jillian said quietly. "I just hope that doesn't mean you and I won't stay friends."

"Then you forgive me for not telling you?"

"Not in a minute." She heard the bell ring over the door and the excited chatter of children as they oohed and aahed over the new guinea pigs. "But I will let you buy me lunch to make up for your little surprise."

"Hannah's on the square?"

"One o'clock. Don't be late."

"See you then. Oh, and Jillian?"

"Yes?"

"He always asks about you."

"I don't want to hear this. Not one more word!"

"Okay. Tomorrow at one. Bye."

The line went dead. Two excited little faces strained to see the new arrivals through the glass cage. With a rub to her temples and a stretch of her tense neck, Jillian pasted on a smile and prepared to explain all there was to know about domesticated South American rodents of the *Caviinae* family.

By the end of the day, Jillian was ready to move to another town. Perhaps Tyler needed a new pet store. Or maybe Longview. But with her luck, her well-meaning friends and neighbors would simply follow her there, hopeful and inquisitive looks on their faces when they asked about *him*.

Until February fourteenth, her life had been so well-ordered, so predictable. The older customers and mothers with young children came by as soon as the store opened. The lunch "rush" didn't amount to much in Scottsville but occurred just the same. The after school visitors, who mostly wanted to browse. One customer who would come by as soon as she'd counted the cash in the register. Lunch every week with Brenda at Hannah's Cafe across the town square.

And then there were her evenings. Dinner on Mondays, Wednesdays, and Fridays with her dad. Reading trade journals and veterinary digests on a regular basis. Balancing her personal and business checkbooks once a month. An occasional decorating project in her apartment, or a fix-up repair at the house where she'd grown up and Dad still lived.

An occasional date with someone who, according to her meddling friends and neighbors, was "just perfect" for her.

They never were, she thought with a sigh as she locked the door and flipped the sign to closed. She'd probably had two dozen dates in the last ten years with men who had come highly recommended by Dr. Taylor's receptionist, or Brenda, or the aging Gardner sisters, or a half dozen other unofficial Scottsville dating consultants.

She knew, in those dark corners of her mind she didn't want to explore, that she'd compared those other men to the Brad Patterson she remembered from her youth. He'd been witty, intelligent, sensitive, and sexy as hell—even as an eighteen year old. Her first love . . . how could she ever forget him, or fail to measure other men by his standard?

Which was probably why she'd never done more than kiss one of those "just perfect" men goodnight—and goodbye.

A loud meow from her cat, Cleo, reminded her that it was time for her dinner. "You're my date for tonight," Jillian said as she picked up the white cat with the calico tail. With her other hand, she snagged the deposit envelope to drop by the bank later.

Just as she was about to head upstairs to her apartment above the store, a rapid, faint knock sounded on the front door. She thought about ignoring the summons; surely they couldn't see her in the rear of the darkened shop. Unfortunately, she could see them—at least the soft, pale lavender curls of Millicent Gardner, Greta's naturally gray hair, and the tall, robust figure of Hannah Bryant standing behind the elderly sisters. All of them were clearly outlined by the dusky late afternoon sunset.

The temperature was too cold for the three ladies to be out and about on a casual visit—which meant they had something up their sleeve. Jillian wasn't the least bit unsure about why the ladies were visiting.

"Sorry, Cleo. Dinner is postponed. Feel free to start on hors d'oeuvres without me."

Her cat meowed and disappeared up the stairs. "Chicken," Jillian murmured at Cleo's retreating figure.

After tucking the cash bag beneath the register, Jillian quickly unlocked the door. Three chilly women hurried inside.

"What a norther!" Hannah exclaimed as Jillian locked the door against any more visitors. "That wind will chill you through."

"It certainly blew in quickly," Millicent agreed, pulling her tweed wool coat close around her neck.

"We didn't have any customers at the bakery this afternoon," Greta complained. "How about you, Jillian? Did anyone come by your store?"

"Just a few," she replied, knowing which customers they wanted to know about. *Him.* The one who'd bought the puppy he had yet to claim.

"Brad Patterson said he was going to bring his computer to the bakery and work there," Millicent said in a tone that would have done any four year old proud.

"I'm sure the weather kept him away," Hannah said. "I was half expecting him to come by for lunch with you and Brenda."

Jillian hid a shudder. She didn't want to visualize Brenda and Brad sitting across from her at lunch, expectant, encouraging looks coming from her best friend, suggestive, challenging ones coming from the prodigal brother. "No, that wasn't even discussed."

"I remember when the three of you used to come by for cookies," Millicent said, her mood instantly lightened by the memory. "You had the cutest red curls."

Jillian, who had hated her carrot-top hair as a child, smiled as kindly as possible to the older woman.

"The three of you were inseparable," Greta added.

"That was a long time ago."

"Seems like just yesterday," the more devious of the two bakery owners observed.

"Seems like an eternity to me," Jillian replied, crossing her arms over her chest, "and it will be another eternity before you see me sharing a meal, a cookie, or anything else with Brad Patterson."

"Now, what happened was a long time ago. He's a responsible father now," Greta said.

He'd been such a good drama student in high school that he

could make almost anyone believe he was sincere. Of course, he might really be a good father, but that wasn't her concern—just like she didn't care if he seemed intent on challenging her to a battle of wits and will. "Fine. He can keep on being a responsible father. That doesn't mean I have to socialize with him."

"Do you remember the time you had that Valentine party at the high school? We made red velvet cakes and decorated them with white cream frosting and red roses," Millicent said in a dreamy voice. "You two sure made a cute couple."

Jillian closed her eyes and recited a quick prayer for patience. Why was everyone so interested in her love life—or lack thereof? Why did everyone assume that she would inevitably be drawn to her old flame? Just because he was still attractive and newly available didn't mean she had any interest in pursuing a relationship. Other than being polite in public and providing a puppy for Jeremy, she had no intention of being around Brad Patterson any more than necessary. She'd spent the last six years building her business. She loved the pet store, her rather unexciting social life, her dad, and even the town busybodies who wanted to see her matched up with a man who had chosen a different path years ago.

"Millicent, Greta, Hannah," she said as gently as possible, gathering their chilled hands together, "we aren't a couple any more. We are never going to be a couple again. Do you understand? Please don't get any ideas that he and I are getting back together. It's just not going to happen."

The bell over the door jingled mid-morning the next day as Jillian tried to figure out the new version of her accounting program.

"Upgrade, my foot," she muttered as she banged on the enter key, trying to get out of the frustrating loop that wouldn't let her answer the question the way she wanted. "Stupid machine."

"Personal computers don't possess any intelligence on their own," a deep voice from the doorway advised.

Jillian jumped, shaking her already wobbly office chair. Brad

Patterson lunged forward, steadying the back with one hand as he grasped her arm with the other.

"I'm fine," she asserted, trying to push away from him without being too obvious. His grip on her didn't lesson, his warm hand as firm as a wide, black leather collar with lethal-looking metal studs.

"You looked as though you might topple over."

"Well, I didn't," she said defensively, pulling from his grasp with a twist of her shoulder.

"A simple thank you would have been enough."

Her mouth opened in wonder at his nerve. Why, if he hadn't sneaked up on her . . . She snapped her jaw shut, narrowing her eyes at his smug expression. "You surprised me on purpose."

"Did not," he said, smiling in that infuriating way he'd learned sometime in the last eleven years.

"I'm not going to argue with you. If that's what you came for, you might as well go home."

"I can't do that," he said, leaning against the door frame. "Believe it or not, I had a more important reason for coming here than scaring you out of your pants."

"You did not . . . And quit making those ridiculous innuendoes. You're just saying those things to irritate me."

"Is it working?"

She glared at him, intent on getting out of her office. She felt trapped, toyed with like a mouse whose nice little home was being invaded by a big, fat, hairy paw of a hungry cat. Too bad she didn't have an equally large trap she could spring on the unwanted invader. The memory of an old Tom and Jerry cartoon popped into her head, and she nearly smiled as she put Brad Patterson's handsome face onto the animated feline who got his comeuppance from the clever mouse.

"Cat got your tongue?"

The irony was too much. Jillian burst into laughter, brushing by Brad with a wave of her hand and tears of mirth turning him into a wavering kaleidoscope of colors.

"What's so funny?" he asked, following her into the store.

"Nothing," she said, trying to control the chuckles that still escaped. She wiped her eyes at the cash register and turned to face her childhood adversary. "I couldn't possibly explain."

"Are you making fun of me, Jillian?" He appeared cautious,

looking at her from beneath lowered eyelids, his brows drawn together in an exaggerated frown.

"You seem to be doing great on your own. Do you need any help in that area, Brad?" She answered his question with one of her own, knowing how that would irritate him. Fine. He was trying his best to get to her, too.

"Age hasn't improved your disposition," he accused with a frown.

"Hasn't improved your sense of humor either," she shot back.

"Daddy! I found the one I want!"

Jeremy's excited chatter stopped the building tension as effectively as a splash of cold water. Jillian's surprise at seeing the boy was nearly as great as her startled reaction to his dad. This time, however, she wasn't in a position to topple from a chair.

"Did you see all the puppies?" she asked, squatting down so she was eye level with the enthusiastic youngster. He looked so much like Brad that her heart did a little skip. Bright gray-blue eyes, untamed dark brown hair, and the hint of a man's bold, handsome face.

"Yes!" he answered with barely contained energy. He looked as though he might jump up and down any moment. Jeremy's father had certainly learned to contain all his vitality, channeling it into a sexual intensity that couldn't be ignored.

When she and Brad were children, she didn't have a clue that one day they'd be lovers. Twenty years ago in Scottsville, life was all innocent fun and the occasional scolding for getting caught after a silly prank. Of course she didn't know then that one day, Brad would have a son who was his spitting image. Or that he'd go off and marry someone else—someone who would be the mother of his child.

Her laughter over the cartoon forgotten, her mood shattered by the memories that refused to stay where they belonged, she could only stare at the little boy who wanted a puppy. She absolutely refused to wonder whether he missed his mother, or where she was, or if Brad missed her too.

"Which puppy do you like, Jeremy?"

"Come on," he said, tugging on her hand. "I'll show you!"

She smiled, rising from the floor, feeling much older than

twenty-eight. Jeremy's mood was too infectious to resist. He pulled her toward the puppy's enclosure, his shorter legs pumping. Jillian followed, hoping again she could push thoughts of Brad out of her mind.

"This one!" Jeremy exclaimed, pointing to a wiggley bundle of black, brown, and white.

"Oh, he's a cutey," Jillian agreed, watching Jeremy reach over the low fencing to pet the Beagle pup. Almost immediately, another Beagle emerged from the brightly painted "doghouse" in the middle of the pen and ran toward the commotion, begging for equal attention.

"Hey, which one is that?" Jeremy asked as the two puppies jumped and whined for attention.

"That's his sister. She's very nice too."

"Oh," Jeremy said, frowning. "I didn't know there were two puppies just alike."

"I had four Beagle puppies," Jillian explained, "but I sold the other two last week. These two are waiting for good homes."

"As long as it's okay with your father, you can have the little girl puppy if you like her better."

"I like them both," Jeremy said, still obviously in deep thought. "Daddy?"

"Yes, son."

Jillian almost jumped again at the sound of Brad's voice, close behind her. She'd been watching the puppies and Jeremy so intently that she hadn't heard him approach. The man was making a habit of sneaking up on her.

"If I take the boy puppy home, the other puppy will be lonely."

"She'll find a good home with another boy or girl," Brad explained.

"But they're brothers and sisters! I think they'll be sad."

"No, they won't. They'll adjust just fine."

"What's adjust?" Jeremy asked, looking at Jillian.

"Your dad means that they'll miss each other at first, but before long they'll be just fine. Whichever puppy you want will have a great time with you."

The little boy shook his head. "No, I want both of them. Daddy, can I have two puppies?"

"I think one puppy is enough, Jeremy. After all, this is your first pet. Let's not overdo it."

"But Daddy, they'll be lonesome. I just know they will. See how they're licking each other on their ears? Please, Daddy?"

"I don't think—"

"But Daddy, I don't know which one I want. They look the same, and I don't want to make one of them sad."

Jillian watched several barely discernible emotions flit across Brad's face. Love for his son. Panic that he might say the wrong thing—or end up with two puppies instead of one. Fear that Jeremy wouldn't understand if he said no. She could almost feel the war raging inside him over an issue which would be simple for most parents to decide. However, given Brad's divorce and the move to Scottsville, she imagined he was a little more sensitive to separating two puppies—and disappointing a small boy.

"Jeremy, why don't you play with the puppies and let me talk to your father about dogs. We'll be back in just a few minutes, okay?"

"Okay," he said in a less than enthusiastic tone. However, as she watched, he reached both hands inside and immediately shrieked as the puppies jumped toward his wiggling fingers. As she turned away and caught Brad's gaze, she heard Jeremy's shrieks of delight.

"What are you up to, Jillian Snow?" Brad asked as he followed her down the narrow aisle toward her office.

"You're a suspicious man," she accused lightly.

He cupped her elbow, bringing her to a stop right outside the doorway. Her heart pounding, she turned and faced the last man she'd expected to move back home.

"Only where you're concerned," he replied in a low, deep voice that sent shivers down her spine. "Why is that, Jillian?"

Chapter Three

"Maybe because you don't trust me—which of course, doesn't make any sense. If anyone should be mistrusted, it's you."

"I haven't done anything . . . lately."

"True, but you've only been in town a few days."

"You love to sink the fangs in, don't you?"

"Only with you."

His eyes narrowed, he studied her as she raised her chin and glared defiantly back. His Jillian hadn't changed much, after all. She still had the temper to match her red hair.

And he still had the urge to kiss her senseless.

"Let's call a truce."

"Not until you admit why you were suspicious of me. I was just trying to discuss your son's concerns over separating the two puppies."

Brad rubbed a hand over his face, conceding defeat. "I apologize for assuming you had an ulterior motive. I should have realized that where animals are concerned, you're always straightforward."

"That's right. And you should also realize that I'd never hurt a child, either."

"Not even to get back at his father?"

"Not even that—although the temptation is there," she said, tilting her chin up once more.

Temptation? She didn't know the meaning of the word. The desire to kiss his way down her neck grew to an overwhelming urge as he watched her pulse beat rapidly just above her emerald green, jewel-necked sweater. He raised his hand, intent on touching the smooth, pale skin of her throat.

Her eyes widened as she stepped back, right into her office. "I . . . we should . . ." She swallowed, a fascinating sight as he imagined his lips moving over that same bare area.

"Should we?" he whispered.

"Talk about Jeremy," she blurted out.

"Jeremy?"

"Yes. And the puppies. And—"

"Are you changing the subject?"

"No," she said, running her fingers over the keyboard. Even as she denied his suspicion, he could see she was avoiding him. His eyes, his touch.

She wouldn't be working so hard to stay away if she didn't care. The knowledge caused him to smile, despite the fact she'd thwarted his most recent advances. He'd go along for now. After all, he was back in Scottsville to stay.

"Do you think he really wants both of those puppies?" he asked.

"I think most children want what they ask for ... at that moment. The question is, will he want both of them in a week, or a month? Puppies can be very demanding, and they grow up so soon. By Christmas, they'll be full grown dogs who need to be walked and cleaned up after."

"We have a big yard."

"True, but they'll still need attention."

"Would they really be happier together?" Brad asked. "I mean, that way, they'll have each other for company when Jeremy is away at school ... or somewhere else."

Jillian's eyes reflected a brief emotion, so fleeting Brad couldn't identify the source. But then she asked, "Like visiting his mother?"

He took a deep breath, his mind racing at the implications of Jillian's pained look and her reference to Karen. Did the fact he had an ex-wife bother Jillian, or was it because of Jeremy? Jillian had never married, for whatever reason. Lack of appropriate men, shyness, or just plain old stubbornness. That didn't matter; he was simply glad she hadn't given her heart irrevocably to another man.

"Yes, he'll visit his mother in the summer and some weekends. She's pretty busy with her career, though, so—"

"You don't have to explain. I shouldn't have asked."

Brad shrugged. "It's no big deal. I'm not suffering from some post-divorce syndrome. We agreed to live separate lives."

"It's none of my business."

"No, but I don't mind explaining. I don't have any big secrets in my life, Jillian."

"Really? You certainly kept moving back to Scottsville a secret."

"It was a surprise, not a secret."

"Six of one, half-dozen of the other."

"Okay, we're back to clichés. How about discussing the puppies? What's your opinion of whether they'd be happier together than if they were separated?"

"I think they'd be happier, but I don't want to put pressure on you to take both dogs."

"Why, Jillian, that's very thoughtful. I didn't know you cared," he joked.

She curled down one side of her mouth and narrowed her eyes. "I was thinking of the puppies. I want them to go to a *good* home."

"I have a good home."

"I suppose I'll have to take your word for that."

"Nonsense. Come over and see. I wouldn't want you to agree to let the puppies go just anywhere."

"I don't need to visit your house."

"But I'd like for you to see the place. Besides, we need to puppy-proof the place. Who knows what kinds of dangers lurk in my laundry room? And I'd like to have your expert opinion on what kind of mischief they might get into—like chewed up furniture or broken knickknacks."

"You have knickknacks?" she asked, disbelief warring with humor in her voice.

"A few," he said, going for a mysterious yet defensive tone that would fuel her curiosity. "Come over and see."

"Brad, that isn't a good idea and you know it."

"No, I don't. I think it's an excellent idea. After all, you promised personal service in selecting a puppy or kitten and getting it settled. That's all I'm talking about."

"Why don't I believe you?" she asked in a skeptical tone.

"You're just a suspicious person," he offered with a shrug. "Besides, I know you'll want to see for yourself what type of knickknacks a divorced father has. Admit it; you'll be wondering what my house looks like, how I'm living, from now on. The puppies give you the perfect excuse."

Her mouth dropped open in a perfect "O." "I happen to

know where you're living, and I have no reason to be curious about your furniture.''

"Come on, Jillian. This is Brad. I know you better than that.''

"Not any longer.''

"I don't think you've changed very much.''

"You don't know," she said, shaking her head. "We were just teenagers.''

"Yes, but we were pretty mature in a lot of ways," he responded, remembering very clearly how womanly Jillian had been at seventeen, and how she'd made him feel ten feet tall and indestructible.

"That was a long time ago," she said, echoing that familiar sentiment.

"Now that I've moved back to town, it feels like yesterday.''

"Since I never left, it feels like forever.''

He looked at her, unsure what to say. He'd hurt her. Fate had interrupted her dreams, but was she bitter? She was right about one thing; she had changed in some important ways. Deep down inside, though, he believed she was still the same feisty, intelligent girl he'd fallen in love with as a boy.

"Come to the house. Let's see how Jeremy acts with both puppies, then I'll follow whatever advice you have on keeping just one or both.''

"I can't leave the store, Brad. I have responsibilities here.''

"I know that. Why don't we come by for you as soon as you close shop? That way you don't have to bother with transporting the puppies yourself.''

"I don't know . . .''

"Come on, Jillian. I dare you. Heck, I double-dare you.''

"No fair. We're talking about a potentially bad idea here.''

"No, we're not. I'm just offering you the chance to see where the puppies might live. Besides, I know you want to spend some time with me.''

"You are so conceited.''

"Confident, Jillian. There's a difference.''

"Only in your mind," she said, rolling her eyes. She tilted her head to the side, stared at the ceiling, and finally relented. "Okay, I'll come by. But I'm not staying long. I'm only doing this for Jeremy and the puppies.''

"With such a gracious acceptance, how can I question your motives? Would six o'clock be about right?"

"Yes. You can pick out the puppy food, bowls, and a collar now if you'd like."

"Part of the deal, hmm?"

"Yes. You paid for it," Jillian said.

"All for a good cause."

"The Brad Patterson School for the Performing Arts?"

"You think I'm performing?"

She shrugged. "I think you want me and everyone else to believe you're back to stay."

"And you don't believe I am?"

She shook her head. "I believe you think you are, but you were in a hurry to leave once before. You hardly ever came home, and then you settled somewhere else. Why would you want to live here now?"

"Jillian, I may have made some bad decisions when I was younger, but I take being a father very seriously. I want Jeremy to have the kind of childhood I did."

"Times have changed."

"Not so much in Scottsville."

"Exactly. We're boring. For someone who's used to Houston—"

"It's a welcome change." He finished the sentence for her before she could continue with more of her suspicions.

"Okay, Brad," she said, spreading her arms. "I don't know what you're going to do. Again, that's your business. I'm not even sure why we're having this conversation."

He knew, but he wasn't about to tell her. "We'll see you around six," he said, pushing away from the doorframe.

"I'll be there," she said, straightening her spine.

He nodded toward the computer and smiled. "Maybe I can offer my services to help with your software problems."

Jillian frowned. "I'm not sure anyone can help. The darned thing is possessed."

Brad laughed. "I'll bring by my exorcism tools and we'll see what happens."

She fought a smile, but her inherent good nature won through. "I'm sure I just need to read the manual one more time."

"Well, if you need some expert help . . ."

"I'll call the store where I bought it."

"Ouch," he said, clutching his chest. "If you're going to insult me, I'm leaving."

Jillian laughed. "I'll see you at six."

She was surprised by Brad's house. She wasn't sure what she'd expected, but she had assumed his tastes would run to the more modern, more urban. After all, he'd lived in Houston and worked with computers. He'd been married to a professional woman who, Jillian knew from a conversation with Brenda several years ago, was more familiar with a microwave than a gas stove.

However, Brad's sparsely furnished home contained a few choice antiques and lots of bare walls and floors just waiting to be filled. In the living room, only an oak sideboard rested against the far wall, at right angles to the marble-fronted fireplace. The wide mantle begged for photos in silver, pewter, and gold frames. The freshly refinished wood floors craved a colorful hooked rug, perhaps in a cabbage rose pattern. She stood in the wide doorway and saw the room unfolding, piece by piece, as she mentally added two chairs beside the hearth, occasional tables, and a soft, cushiony couch.

"Penny for your thoughts."

Jillian jumped as Brad's voice wafted over her shoulder like a heat wave, startling her from her daydreams. Or nightmare, she thought, rubbing her arms as she looked out the wide windows into the cold darkness.

She gave him one quick glance before deciding that focusing on the room was much safer. Decorating Brad's house, even in her mind, was as stupid as agreeing to come over here to "get the puppies settled." He'd always had dogs as a boy. She knew Brad could manage to fill food dishes, a water bowl, and spread out bedding for the two Beagles.

But he'd caught her in a weak moment, bringing up their shared past, talking about puppies and children, pressuring her into honoring the donation she'd made at the Valentine's Day charity auction.

Not to mention the trademark Brad Patterson sex appeal, she thought with a sigh.

"I'm just wondering where the rest of your furniture is," she finally replied, giving her arms another rub.

"Back in Houston, I imagine. It was more suited for the condo than a Victorian-style house in Scottsville."

"Lots of chrome and black leather?"

"Let's just say that my ex's tastes are different than mine."

"You must have had something in com—" She almost clapped a hand over her mouth. "Forget I said that. It's none of my business."

He stepped closer. She felt his warm breath over her shoulder, teasing her neck. "You seem to be saying that a lot. Why don't you just admit that you're curious about me?"

She heard the humor in his voice, but wasn't about to give in to Brad's persistence. "Because I'm not," she explained in her defense, taking a step into the living room. "I was making conversation. Trying to be polite . . . except I asked too many questions."

"Don't fib, Jillian. You're not good at it."

She turned to face him. "You don't know what I'm good at any longer. I may have developed entirely new talents in the past eleven years."

"Really?" he replied, raising an eyebrow. "Would you like to demonstrate?"

"Absolutely not!"

Brad laughed.

Jeremy burst into the hallway, squealing in delight as the two puppies chased him. He careened into his dad's legs, grasping Brad's jeans with a giggle.

"Jeremy, what did I tell you about running in the house?" Brad asked as he steadied his excited son with two large hands on the boy's shoulders.

"No running in the house," Jeremy repeated, his voice still full of laughter. The puppies didn't help, nipping at his sneakers and pant's legs.

"Stop that right now!"

Brad, Jeremy, and both Beagles froze as they looked at her. She almost giggled herself at the sight of four pairs of wide eyes.

"Now Jeremy," she said more gently, "the puppies cannot play that way in the house. They'll knock over the furniture," she explained, looking around the mostly bare rooms, "or at least they will as soon as your dad gets all moved in. And they could hurt themselves if something heavy fell on them, right?"

Jeremy nodded.

"So we have to teach them to behave when they're in the house. You can run and play with them outside, when your dad says it's okay."

"Daddy, can I go outside?" the boy immediately asked.

"Not tonight, son. We need to make the puppies feel at home in the laundry room, remember? What were you supposed to be doing?"

"Putting an old blanket on the floor," Jeremy answered in a smaller voice.

"I'll help you, okay? Then we can order some pizza for dinner."

"Great!"

"Well, I'll be going . . ." Jillian said, taking a deep breath. Brad apparently had everything under control once again. She reminded herself that he didn't really need her help. She was just here because he'd appealed to both her curiosity about his house and her sense that she should honor her word.

And he had some bizarre notion that he could torment her into admitting some lingering affection for him. Well, he could wait until those puppies were full grown. Until Jeremy was full grown. She wasn't going to admit to anything that foolish. Besides, it wasn't true. She absolutely had no affection for Brad Patterson, lingering or otherwise.

"Don't be silly," he said, interrupting her retreat toward the front door. "We have lots to do. You've got to stay for supper."

"No, I don't."

"Jeremy has lots to learn. You want the puppies to be well cared for, don't you?"

"I think you're perfectly capable of telling your son everything he needs to know about feeding and caring for them."

"Do you know how long it's been since I've had a pet?" Brad asked, walking up and looping an arm around her back.

She tried to step away, but he came with her, smiling all the while. "Stop that," she whispered, so Jeremy wouldn't hear.

"Come on, Jillian. I want you to look around until the pizza gets here. There might be hidden dangers in this old house."

In her opinion, the only danger beneath this roof was the owner.

"I told you I couldn't stay long."

"The pizza place is very prompt. I'll call right now. Would you watch Jeremy and the puppies while I take care of that order?"

Before she could answer, he strode away, heading for the kitchen.

But I have to go, she longed to say. The words froze on her lips as she looked down at Brad's son.

"Want to come see my room?" he asked innocently.

Jillian smiled, unable to resist a child, especially one as charming as Jeremy. "Sure, but shouldn't we put the blanket down and the food out first?"

"I want them to see my room, too."

"Okay, but you have to let them know they can't stay there with you at night. It's important that they have their own place to sleep."

"Why?"

"Because puppies need lots of rest, and if they stay with you, they'll want to play." Just like playful little boys needed lots of sleep.

"I like to play," he said as he took her hand and led her up the stairs.

Jillian smiled at his chatter. Hand in hand, puppies struggling up the steps behind them, she went upstairs to see Jeremy's room.

"Really, I have to go," she said an hour and a half later. She'd seen Jeremy's room, Brad's room—his very sparse furniture and huge bed—and the rest of the house before the pizza arrived. They'd put the Beagles in the laundry room during dinner amid loud yaps of protest. After pizza and diet soda, they'd "puppy-proofed" the house and stressed the importance of safety to Jeremy. He'd taken it well, as responsible as a much older child when Jillian explained how his new pets could never be allowed to chew on electrical cords or telephone lines.

And he'd asked her to tuck him in before his dad came in

to tell him goodnight. The recent memory caused a curious lump in Jillian's throat.

"You were great with Jeremy," Brad said, as if he could read her thoughts.

"He's a good kid. I don't know where he gets it, but—"

"Watch it," Brad warned, smiling as he closed the pizza box.

"So, I suppose there's no doubt that both puppies will be staying." She picked up her purse and car keys, ready to make a dash for the door now that they were all alone without even a pizza box between them.

"I think that was settled long ago," Brad replied, crossing his arms over his chest. "Thanks for coming out and helping us with everything."

"It's all part of that personal service," she said lightly, giving him what she hoped was a very impersonal smile. "Goodnight, Brad."

"I haven't paid you for the other puppy."

"Oh." She really wanted to leave. Now. Before he tried another of his sophisticated seduction moves. Not that she was wavering . . . but it had been so long since she'd felt anything close to the excitement that she remembered so well.

"I'll write you a check. We can stop by my office on the way to the front door."

He motioned for her to precede him into the darkened hallway. Darn the man. He must know that she wanted to leave. However, she wouldn't stay in business long if she gave away *two* puppies, food, and accessories.

"Which way?" she asked as they walked toward the front.

"Right here," Brad said behind her. He opened the double paneled doors, then flipped on the light.

Finally, a room that was fully furnished! A long credenza holding two computers stretched along one wall. A desk faced the room, but stood in the area of the turret, giving him a good view in three directions if he swung his chair around. The surface of his desk held stacks of papers, a cache of pens and a small pile of unopened envelopes. Several file cabinets looked as though he was in the process of filing them from boxes placed haphazardly on the hardwood floors.

"Brenda said you were working from home."

"That's right. It's a good setup for me because I can be around Jeremy during the day until he goes to school this fall."

"With a four year old and two puppies, I don't expect you'll get much work done."

Brad smiled as he searched the desktop for his checkbook. "I work in spurts. Jeremy still takes a long nap, and you'd be surprised how much I can get done in two hours."

"What do you do exactly?"

"That would take a while to explain. How much?"

"How much what?"

"For the puppy and things."

"Oh. Let's say fifty."

"Are you sure? They look purebred." He located the checkbook and began writing.

"They are. I'll have to get you the papers. There's a local family who breeds them. They're not champions or anything, but come from good stock. More important, they were raised in a family, around children. You shouldn't have any problem with adjustment."

"I didn't expect any. I assumed you wouldn't get your animals from a puppy mill."

"Of course not! I hate those places. They should be outlawed."

"I agree. Now, when do you think you'll have time for me to explain?"

"Explain what?"

"What I do for a living."

"Forget I asked," she said quickly. "I was being nosy again."

"Nonsense," he answered easily. "I'd love to tell you about my work." He looked up and smiled again. "How about coffee tomorrow morning at Hannah's? I'll describe the exciting world of software development."

Jillian flashed him a skeptical look. "Thanks, but I think I'll pass. I'm not real happy with computers right now."

"Oh, yes. The possessed CPU in your office. I did offer to help."

"And I politely turned you down."

He looked at her for what seemed an eternity, until she felt like shuffling her feet and twisting the keys in her hand. "Is that what you did?"

"Yes," she said, her voice sounding breathless. "And I've really got to be going."

Brad placed the check in her outstretched hand. "Are you sure?"

"Yes." She folded the check and stuffed it in her jacket pocket. "Thanks for the pizza."

"My pleasure," he said, coming around the desk until he stood before her. "I'll walk you to your car."

"That's not necessary."

"I'm trying to be a gentleman."

"Is that what you're trying to do?"

He smiled. "Absolutely."

She gave him another skeptical look. "Let's not get into an argument about whether I believe you."

"That's fine with me. I just want to walk you to your car."

"Oh, all right. I have to go."

"Not used to these exciting, late nights?" he joked as they walked out of his office.

"My idea of an exciting evening is testing the water in the fish tanks."

"Jillian, you don't get out enough," he said with a chuckle as he opened the front door.

"You may not remember this, but there's not a lot to do in Scottsville after they roll the sidewalks up at dusk."

"Dates?"

"Now you're getting too personal," she said lightly as she reached her car. The blue Norther that had blown in yesterday kept the temperatures cold and the night air clear. A brisk wind whistled through the pine trees and scattered dried leaves across Brad's lawn.

He touched her arm. All thoughts of cold temperatures skittered from her mind as she began to glow like the heat lamp over the iguana cage.

"Be serious for a minute, Jillian. Tell me if you're dating anyone."

"Why?"

"Because I'm trying not to ask Brenda too many questions," he said, stepping closer, blocking the wind. "Because I want to know.'' His head dipped lower. ''Because I wouldn't want to kiss you if you were serious about another man.''

She parted her lips to tell him that her personal life was none of his business. That he shouldn't ask Brenda, and he shouldn't pry. But all that came out was a tiny moan that he must have taken as an invitation.

The next thing she knew, his mouth settled over hers, warm and firm and sure, tasting of spicy pizza and wicked delights.

And eleven years melted away with the heat of his kiss.

Chapter Four

Brad tried to go slowly, but as soon as his lips touched Jillian's, he felt as though they'd never been apart. All the passion of youth, combined with the thrill of discovery, pushed him to deepen the kiss. When he felt her relax against him and part her lips, he pulled her closer and slanted his mouth over hers. She responded with equal desire until they were both breathless, breaking apart only when they couldn't draw in any more air.

Jillian's moan of protest brought him back for another taste of what he'd missed this past eleven years. But instead of her welcoming his kiss, she turned aside, pushing gently against his chest.

''No, Brad. We . . . we can't. We shouldn't,'' she said, her voice thin and shaky in the darkness.

''Why not, Jilly? This feels so right.''

She shook her head as they stood close together, her warmth seeping through his shirt and jacket, her scent swirling around him with a heady fragrance more intoxicating than the finest brandy.

''I'm not getting involved with you. Not again. I'm not that stupid.''

Her whispered words hurt more than he wanted to admit, even to himself. ''Our involvement wasn't stupid. Don't try to say that what we had was a big mistake,'' he said, rubbing her arms, doing whatever he could to hold her a little longer.

"Wasn't it? It sure felt like it when you went away." He heard the bitterness in her voice and didn't blame her for what she was feeling. He had hoped that her anger and pain would have lessened, but he understood why she didn't trust him.

"How often can I say I'm sorry?" he said gently. "I didn't mean to hurt you. I just wanted you to be there with me, like we'd always planned, and when you couldn't, I acted like an ass."

"You knew I couldn't go off and leave my father after his accident," she said in a breaking voice that tore at his heart. "You knew that, and yet you practically taunted me with the excitement of attending Texas A & M, your new friends, the weekend parties. How was I supposed to compete with that, Brad?"

He stiffened, holding her still when she tried to pull away. "I never thought that you were competing with my life at college."

She made a noise that could have been a sob or a bitter laugh; he couldn't tell which one. When he tried to pull her close for a hug, she twisted away. The light from the porch showed a sheen of tears in her wide eyes as the wind teased curling locks of hair around her face. "Don't cry, Jilly," he whispered.

"I'm not crying. Don't think that I am. After we broke up . . . then, I cried. I needed your support, Brad, but you weren't there for me. I learned I didn't need you. I grew up." She pushed her hair back with a hand that shook ever so slightly.

"I was a stupid kid. That doesn't mean our love was stupid."

"Were we in love, Brad? Or were we just a couple of hormone-crazed teenagers who didn't know any better? It seems to me that you discovered a whole new world once you got away from Scottsville."

"Do you really want me to tell you about that first semester at school? I'll stand out here and talk all night if it will help."

She shook her head again, sending her hair flying around her face again. "No, that's not what I want. I don't want to talk about it at all."

"We should talk. Maybe not here in the cold, maybe not tonight—"

"Or maybe not ever," she said, taking a step back. "I'm not going through that again."

"I'm not asking you to. Why can't we start over? We're not teenagers any longer."

"No, Brad. I know what's best for me, and my life doesn't include you or your son. I'm happy with what I have, what I've built for myself. I don't need you."

"I don't want you to need me," he lied, knowing that he wanted her to need his touch, his kisses, his body. "There's a big difference between need and desire."

"Then let me make myself even more clear; I'm not going to have an affair with you," she said as she plunged her hands into her pockets.

"I don't remember asking," he said defensively, getting angry that she could dismiss everything he offered. He understood why she was hurting. He'd been a jerk when he was eighteen, but he wasn't a teenager any longer. The time was right for them to build a relationship as adults, but that obviously wasn't going to happen if Jillian couldn't get past her pain.

"Fine. Just believe what I said, Brad. I'm not going to fall at your feet. Despite what everyone in this town thinks, we are not right for each other."

"How do you know if you won't give us a chance?" he answered, striving for calm and reason when her words made him want to prove how good they could be together . . . again.

"I don't have to drink poison to know it can kill me."

"I'm not poison, Jilly," he said softly, his earlier anger melting away when he realized how desperately she was trying to build defenses against getting involved.

She looked away, biting her lip as though she was keeping herself from saying something she knew she'd regret. Finally, she pushed her hair back and glanced at him once more. "I'm going home, Brad. Please don't try to convince me to start any kind of relationship with you."

"I can't agree to that."

"Then I guess you're going to be disappointed."

"I've been disappointed before, Jilly, but not by you."

"And don't call me Jilly. The name's Jillian."

He felt his mouth turn up very slightly as he watched her stride the short distance to her car. Okay, the evening had gone pretty well until he kissed her. Or actually, until he'd tried to kiss her the second time. He should have realized he was pushing her. He should have stopped with just a taste, but he hadn't been in control since that first time they'd made love, twelve years ago this summer, beside Caddo Lake at sunset.

He would try, he swore to himself, to maintain some control around her. He couldn't afford not to . . . not when his goal was to make her see that not only were they right for each other, but they were just perfect together.

Kissing Brad Patterson had to be the worst mistake of her life. Worse than agreeing to go to his house, having pizza with him and his adorable son, then staying far later than she'd planned. Worse even than getting involved with him the first time.

She'd had a good excuse then; she'd been too darn young to know the pitfalls of relationships. She'd been blindly, crazily, in love.

Well, she wasn't in love any longer, she thought as she scrubbed her face. She knew better, and yet she'd let him kiss her.

"Oh, be honest," she said to herself in disgust. "You kissed him back as though you hadn't kissed another man in eleven years."

The only thing her verbal chiding accomplished was to give her a mouthful of soap. She spat the disgusting stuff with little puffs that drew Cleo's attention to the bathroom sink.

"I'm a complete idiot," Jillian told the cat. "I have no common sense any more, you know that?"

Cleo blinked, her ears forward as if she were agreeing to everything Jillian said.

"But not again. I'm not getting involved with him. I learned my lesson tonight, Cleo." Even if the man could kiss like no other . . .

The cat placed one paw on the edge of the sink and meowed.

"No, I'm not going to think about his . . . him," Jillian told the feline. "We have no future. He probably won't even stay in Scottsville. Before long, he'll miss Houston. When he gets tired of pursuing me, he'll try someone else." Except there weren't many single, young women in town.

Of course, the few there were would jump at the chance to date Brad Patterson, like the new librarian, Mandy Thompson. There weren't very many single *men* in town either.

"Oh, why am I thinking about this?" Jillian asked the cat as she threw her washcloth into the sink. "I'm going to bed."

Cleo jumped down from the toilet lid in front of Jillian, then rubbed against her legs. "You and me, kid," she said to the cat before picking up the fluffy bundle of fur and walking into the dark bedroom.

"At least you won't disappoint me, will you, Cleo?" Jillian asked, rubbing the cat's small pointed ears. "You'll never go away and leave me for a bigger litter box or a prettier food dish, will you, Cleo?"

Jillian placed the cat on the foot of the bed, then turned back the covers and slipped between the sheets. They felt as cool as the night air outside. She'd been so cold until Brad . . .

"No," she said aloud. "I'm not going to think about him."

Cleo meowed as if disputing her word.

"I mean it. No more Brad Patterson. He's got his puppies. I've puppy proofed his house. We're even. I don't have to deal with him again."

Cleo meowed again, this time with a little more attitude.

"What do you know?" Jillian said, turning out the light and snuggling into the fat pillow. Cleo padded around, searching for the perfect spot, then settled down for the night against the back of Jillian's knees.

The old place was so quiet that she heard the wind slide around the northwest corner of the building and swirl against the window. Below, the rosebush in the tiny backyard scratched against the wooden siding like a cat asking to go outside. In the bathroom, the steady plop-plop of her leaking bathtub faucet grated on her nerves like the raucous cry of an angry parrot.

She shifted in the bed, bumping against Cleo as she tried to find some elusive comfort. The warming sheets reminded her of *his* heat, *his* touch in the coolness of the February night. Beneath the bare limbs and bright stars, Brad had kissed her as though he really meant it. As though he dreamed of a future where they lived happily ever after in that big old house with the two Beagles and an energetic, bright little boy.

But she couldn't believe he meant it. He was a good actor, that was all. He wanted her to imagine all those things, even if they weren't real. And eventually, he'd leave. He'd go back to his life in the fast lane, to a place she'd never belong.

Jillian grabbed her pillow and plastered it over her head. She refused to lay in the dark and think, distracted by the sounds of the night that never bothered her before.

She refused to cry for Brad Patterson again.

The next morning, before she'd unlocked the front door, Jillian experienced that funny feeling of being watched. Her fingers stilled as she sorted money into the cash register. Her body tensed as she slowly turned to face the door. She looked past the "closed" sign that hung undisturbed at eye level. Her gaze scanned down, past the logos for credit cards and the posted store hours, to a pair of blue-gray eyes and a tousled head of dark brown hair.

Jeremy. He smiled at her, his nose pressed against the glass as his breath fanned out like butterfly wings in the cool morning air.

Cleo walked over to the door and meowed.

"Yes, I know. I'm coming," Jillian said, shutting the cash drawer and grabbing her keys.

Just as she reached the lock, Brad stepped behind his son, blocking the light as effectively as his body had shielded her from the wind last night. Last night. She groaned as she remembered. The worst part was that she'd have to face him again, his son in tow, when she'd vowed to stay away from them forever.

"Good morning, Jeremy," she said cheerfully as she opened the door. She pointedly ignored Brad; as far as she was concerned, he could do without her greeting. "Is anything wrong? Are the puppies okay?"

"Yeah!" Jeremy answered with gusto, walking into the store. "But we need more toys."

"Puppy toys," Brad said with a small, nearly apologetic

smile as he joined his son inside the warm store. "And that's no way to answer Miss Snow."

"Sorry," Jeremy said over his shoulder, heading back to the dog accessory area. "I meant, 'yes, Miss Jillian.'"

"Miss Jillian?"

"I told Jeremy he could call me Miss Jillian last night," she replied defensively. *Go ahead, make a big deal out of it,* she wanted to yell at Brad. Instead, she narrowed her eyes and crossed her arms over her chest.

"I just assumed it was 'Miss Snow' to everyone."

"Not to my friends."

"And Jeremy is a friend?"

"Yes, of course. I hope all my dog owners are friends."

"Then I'm a friend too," Brad said with a sly smile.

"You," Jillian replied, turning her back to him and following Jeremy's footsteps, "are the father of a friend. Hardly the same thing."

Brad chuckled. She imagined him shaking his head, but didn't turn around to see. After all, she'd decided to ignore the man. She'd hoped she could do that by avoiding him altogether, but if that wasn't an option, she'd just pretend he wasn't standing in her store.

Jillian walked quickly down an aisle toward the real pet owner. "What did you need?" she asked, hunkering down beside Jeremy and smiling at the little boy's intent expression.

"We need squeaky toys, and another big rope with a knot in it 'cause they're fighting over the one they have now. Daddy says puppies need things like that to chew on so they won't chew up the furniture."

"That's right." Letting two puppies gnaw on those beautiful antiques would be a shame. But then, the condition of Brad's furniture wasn't her concern. They were *his* antiques. She forced a smile past her wandering thoughts. "You know, Jeremy, the puppies aren't really fighting. They're playing tug-of-war with that rope."

"That's what Daddy said, but I think they need another rope," he said, reaching for the display.

"If it's okay with your father, then I'm sure the puppies will like whatever you pick out. Did you decide on names yet?"

"I'm still thinkin' about it," Jeremy answered, his attention on the various chew toys.

"I suggested Mutt and Jeff, but he didn't care for those." Brad's voice startled her, making her teeter on the balls of her feet. Before she could catch herself, he reached out and grabbed beneath her arms.

"Stop that!"

"I didn't want you to fall." He removed his hands, but stayed right behind her.

"I wouldn't be in any danger of falling if you didn't sneak up behind me," she replied testily, holding herself steady with the fingertips of one hand touching the floor.

"I'm not sneaking around. You're just not listening."

"My hearing is fine."

"Then you must be distracted by something."

She swiveled around and glared up at him. "I'm not distracted at all. You're obviously trying to irritate me."

"And you're obviously trying to pick a fight."

"Daddy, are you going to yell at Miss Jillian? I don't want you to get mad at her. She's my newest friend."

Brad hunkered down beside his son. "I'm not going to yell at Miss Jillian. We were just teasing each other." He turned to look at her, one eyebrow raised. "Isn't that right?"

"Absolutely," she lied. Boy, was she going to have some explaining to do when she got to the pearly gates. She'd been forced into more fibs this last week than in the past ten years combined.

"We've known each other a long time, Jeremy. Miss Jillian and I used to play together with Aunt Brenda."

"We used to do a lot of *teasing* back then too," Jillian added. More like guerrilla warfare, but there was no reason to tell a four year old that his father had been one hell-raiser of a kid. One of his favorite tricks had been to hide in a treehouse his dad had conveniently built in a large mulberry tree in the side yard. To get from the front to the backyards, you had to walk under that tree—and within water balloon distance of the treehouse. Brad had been an expert on those obnoxious missiles. He dropped them from strings, shot them from slingshots, and sometimes simply lofted them through the air. Jillian couldn't count the times she'd been soaked by Brad's favorite prank.

If Jeremy only knew . . .

"That's a pretty suspicious smile. What's going on up there, Jillian?"

She tried to wipe the amusement off her face, but knew she hadn't succeeded. "I was just remembering your favorite way to tease," she answered.

"Are you sure we can talk about that in front of Jeremy?"

Jillian swatted him on the arm. "I'm talking about the treehouse at your parents' house, and the way you used to lie in wait for us girls."

"Oh, that," he said, a grin spreading across his face, revealing a deep dimple she'd once found irresistible. "Yes, I did spend a lot of time up there."

"What's a treehouse, Daddy?" Jeremy asked, all thoughts of puppy toys temporarily forgotten as he focused on the adults' conversation.

"It's like a little house built high up in a tree so you have to climb a ladder to get inside."

"Cool," Jeremy said, mimicking some television show or movie, no doubt. "Can I have one?"

"I suppose we can build a treehouse as soon as the weather gets warmer. I'd freeze to death up in a tree right now."

"Where's your treehouse?" Jeremy asked.

"I'm sure it's long gone," Brad replied, a hint of wistfulness in his voice. "By the time your grandparents sold the house and moved to Harlingen, the treehouse was pretty old."

"Yeah, really old," Jeremy agreed with an overly serious nod of his head.

Jillian laughed. "I'm sure twenty-some years sounds like an eternity to a four year old, but I don't feel that old."

"Neither do I," Brad said, gazing intently into her eyes. "Especially lately. I'm feeling younger all the time."

Jillian felt a rush of heat and awareness surge through her body. She knew her eyes widened; she sucked in a deep breath. Brad's eyes took on a sexy, dreamy look that made her think all kinds of wicked thoughts—like how . . . enthusiastic . . . he'd been as a teenager. How uninhibited they'd been with each other at the lake, in the car, in her bedroom when her parents played bridge on Friday night.

Oh, Lord, what was she thinking? Worse than that, what was

she *feeling?* She quickly decided she didn't want to delve into the sudden rush of sensation, since her total experience with *that* had been with Brad, eleven years ago.

She pushed herself up from the floor. "I've got some . . . things to do," she said as a lame excuse. "Feel free to look around all you'd like, Jeremy. I'm sure you'll find something nice for the puppies."

"But I wanted you to help," the little boy protested.

And I want to run out of here as fast as I can. Instead, she stood with her hands clenched stiffly at her side, her muscles so tight they ached. She wasn't up to a long conversation with a child, explaining what kind of things grown-ups did. Most of all, she wasn't up to any more teasing by his dad.

"Jeremy, Miss Jillian said she had things to do. Let's thank her for the time she spent with us, okay?"

"Thank you, Miss Jillian," Jeremy said politely but with little excitement, turning back to the dog toys.

"You're welcome," she said softly, her eyes locked with Brad's. Why had Brad supported her rapid retreat? For days he'd been trying to corner her. Now he was giving her a gracious way out. The man was full of surprises, but she wasn't sure she wanted to know why he was being kind. The best thing to do was scoot out of there before she said or did something she'd regret later.

If she hadn't already . . .

Brad paid for his son's purchases in cash, noticing how Jillian barely made eye contact. When she did, she glanced away quickly, her color high. As a true redhead, she blushed easily— and thoroughly. He knew that for a fact, having caused several flushes that began with her forehead and traveled the glorious length of her pale, freckled body.

"Later," he said simply after Jeremy thanked her again and made her promise to come back and see the puppies soon. Her eyes had been wide and luminous as he'd taken his son's hand and walked out of the store. Brad wondered how long she stood in that exact spot, staring at the door. Somehow, he knew that's what Jillian would do. Then she'd shake her head and get busy with some task.

But every now and then, her thoughts would return to that moment on the floor, when she'd become aware of him as a man. When he'd used every ounce of willpower he possessed not to topple her onto the linoleum and kiss her senseless.

Jeremy wouldn't have understood that behavior, either.

"Where are we going now?" his son asked as they walked down the sidewalk, away from the car.

"I thought we'd go by Hannah's and get some hot chocolate for you, some coffee for me. She makes the best muffins I've ever tasted."

"What kind of muffins?" Jeremy asked.

The questions continued as they walked around the quiet town square. The chilling wind and cold temperatures from two days ago had retreated north, so the weather was much more pleasant today. Winter remained evident in the bare limbs and brown grass of the small park in the center of the square, but Brad knew from experience that within weeks, green shoots would push through the wet, decaying leaves. Daffodils would bloom almost overnight, and the buds of new growth would adorn each tree.

He's been right to move home, he thought as he pushed open the door of Hannah's cafe and breathed deeply of the wonderful smells of cinnamon and coffee. He greeted the tall, aging queen of cuisine in Scottsville with a hug, then watched as she showed Jeremy each delight in the case. Some of the baked goods came from the Gardner sisters' bakery, but Hannah always made her own muffins, Brad knew. After a thorough inspection of each item, they purchased muffins and two buttery sugar cookies for later, after Jeremy's nap.

As Brad sipped Hannah's strong coffee and watched his son concentrate on carefully unwrapping, then consuming, a huge cinnamon-crumb muffin, Brad's thoughts returned to Jillian . . . and Scottsville. From the window of the cafe, he could see her pet store through the bare trees, across the square.

There were few secrets in a town like this. What wasn't known as a fact was speculated on, producing a short-list of "probables" that rivaled the best a detective agency or gossip rag could produce. Brad knew he and Jillian were bound to be a hot topic of conversation. What he didn't know is how she'd react to continued speculation by her friends and neighbors.

Would she confront them head-on, or would she simmer and stew until she lashed out at the nosy but well-meaning residents?

He didn't know the mature Jillian well enough to answer. But, he realized, he didn't have any control over what "probables" her friends and neighbors would come up with, unless he made an overt move on her. As long as he was fairly circumspect, the most they could do was ask ... and maybe suggest that she should—or shouldn't—go out with him.

Jillian could handle that. She had enough spunk for two people.

"Daddy, you're not eating your cimbaman muffin," Jeremy observed.

Brad blinked his eyes, wondering how long he'd been lost in his thoughts. "I'm sorry, sport. I was just thinking."

"About the puppies?"

Brad smiled. "No, not really, but that's a good thing to think about."

"I want to go home and play with them now. I bet they like their new toys."

"I bet they do too." Brad felt such love for this little boy. Who would have imagined that he'd be a full-time father? Certainly not any of his former classmates at Scottsville High. None of them had looked beyond going off to college. He hadn't either, because he knew what the future held: a scholarship to Texas A & M; a church wedding with Jillian right after graduation; a great job in the ever-changing world of computer software; a house and kids, far into the future maybe. Not marriage to another woman, a condo in Houston, and his own business before he was thirty. Not a son he adored and a divorce he welcomed.

"Let me finish my coffee, then we'll go home."

Jeremy wandered off to look at Hannah's display of model trains, displayed in a large case that always bore the fingerprints of a dozen kids. High above, an engine and several cars traveled along a track built on a ledge just a foot or so from the ceiling. Every now and then a whistle sounded, making Jeremy's attention focus solely on Hannah's whimsical hobby.

Sure that Jeremy couldn't get into any trouble, Brad sipped his coffee and bit into his roll. His mind drifted back to the past. Life hadn't turned out the way he'd expected, but he didn't regret anything . . . except leaving Jillian. She was supposed to have started college with him, gone to veterinary medicine school, and married him when she turned twenty-two. She would have finished school while he built a career, then she would have found a position in a clinic. She'd always loved animals and had a natural ability to sense their needs, calm their fears, and gain their trust.

He would have supported her career, he thought, taking another bite of the soft, fragrant muffin. They would have had children eventually, when they were both ready. They hadn't really discussed life beyond college. As typical of most teens, he supposed, they'd been self-centered. They'd had their individual dreams and each other; what else could they have possibly needed?

"Daddy, are you ready yet?" Jeremy asked impatiently.

Brad mentally shook himself, focusing on his son and not what could—or should—have been. "Sure, sport. Don't forget your cookies."

He bussed his table, as everyone did at Hannah's, then bid her good-bye for now. Jeremy led him quickly back to the car, which was parked near Jillian's store. He glanced inside, but couldn't see anyone due to the lighting. Just as well, he realized. He might be tempted to see her once more, and then Jeremy would get even more upset that they weren't on their way fast enough.

No, he realized as he unlocked the car and settled Jeremy inside, the best thing was to practice a little patience. He wasn't a hard-charging teen anymore, even though he did feel that way when he was around Jillian. They both had respectable lives, responsible careers, and now, very curious neighbors.

Besides, he had Jeremy to consider. As much as Brad wanted to rush into a relationship with Jillian—physical, emotional, or whatever—he had to consider how that would affect his son. So far, Jeremy had adjusted well to the divorce and the move to Scottsville. Sooner or later, he was bound to question why he lived with his dad and saw his mother only on the occasional weekend. He'd want to know if his dad loved him more than his mom did, and why they couldn't just get back together and live in the same house. He'd want his mother to visit Scottsville, and he'd want to take the puppies—or dogs, by then—to her condo in Houston.

Adding a volatile relationship with Jillian onto that already precarious situation was asking for trouble. Brad knew he needed to go slowly, lay some ground rules, make sure they really could work through the past into a lasting love affair. He needed to be sure she could accept Jeremy as a son.

Most of all, Brad had to be certain that this time, he didn't hurt Jillian again. He'd behaved like a jerk, as he'd already confessed, when he was eighteen. Even though *she* hadn't forgiven him, the town seemed to have made the typical excuses. No one outwardly held a grudge. Homecoming had indeed been sweet.

Now he had to keep it that way. Stay balanced, stay focused on his long-term goal—winning Jillian back. He'd realized sometime in the last few years—somewhere along the road to maturity—that no one else could make him as happy as his freckle-faced best friend.

Now he had to convince her that the man of her dreams was a single dad, a divorced man with lots of dreams, a fair amount of talent, and a growing business. But most of all, he was the hell-raising tormentor of her youth, the boy who could aim a mean water balloon and outrun an irate, carrot-headed girl who had legs that went on forever.

How, exactly, he would accomplish his goal was still a mystery.

Chapter Five

During the next several days, Brad and Jeremy came by the store often. Each time, Jeremy claimed the puppies needed new toys, or more food, or new collars. Brad seemed the indulgent dad, shrugging his shoulders and grinning at each of his son's requests.

Jillian had a sneaking suspicion that he was encouraging the boy to visit the store. There was no way two puppies could need everything the Pattersons bought, no way the little Beagles could eat twenty pounds of food in four days.

She began to smile and shake her head in amusement when Brad opened the door for Jeremy. He'd raise an eyebrow, shrug, and follow the boy back to whatever section contained the day's search. Jillian trailed behind, but Brad always lingered beside her as his son shopped. She began to anticipate his warmth, his unique scent, and his quiet humor.

Before long they were talking about everyday things, and she forgot that she wasn't going to get involved with Brad and Jeremy. She tried very hard to remain neutral about any decisions—the blue collar or the red?—and even harder not to show Brad that she'd forgiven him for moving back to town unannounced.

She wasn't ready to forgive him for what happened eleven years ago, but she admitted to herself that the pain had lessened. She no longer experienced the urge, she realized with a chuckle, to bash him in the head when he showed up at the store.

On Friday, one week after the Valentine's charity event, Jillian and Brenda had their regular lunch at Hannah's.

They'd barely taken their chairs before the questions started. "So, how are things going with Brad?" Brenda asked in an innocent, nonchalant tone that didn't fool Jillian for a minute.

"I haven't committed any violence yet, have I?"

"That's hardly the same as getting along."

"Let's just say that he's not as bad as I thought he'd be."

"Oh, come one!" Brenda protested, leaning forward over the Formica-topped table. "I think there's more than indifference going on here. I know there is as far as Brad's concerned."

That remark made Jillian sit up a little straighter, listen a little more acutely. "What do you mean by that?" she casually asked.

"Just that he's been over to my house several times, and Jeremy's always talking about you and the puppies. And Brad's always asking questions about you."

"What kind of questions? I told him not to ask you about me!"

"Have you ever known Brad to follow any advice he didn't agree with?" Brenda asked with a laugh.

Hannah came by with hot tea for Jillian, iced tea for Brenda.

She smiled as she added news of her own. "Brad and that cute little boy of his were in earlier this week. I swear, that child looks just like him when he was little. Sharp as a tack, too."

"I know," Brenda said. "Every time Jeremy comes to my house he asks dozens of questions I can't answer, then tells me he'll ask his dad when he gets home."

Hannah chuckled, then leaned closer in a conspiratorial stance. "Brad seemed to be thinking pretty hard about something while he was having coffee," she said with a wiggle of her neatly penciled eyebrows.

"How do you know?" Brenda asked.

"He barely touched his muffin—and you know how he loves those cinnamon-crumb ones."

Brenda nodded.

"I'm sure he has lots on his mind, especially since he's moved his business and his home," Jillian said as she studied the menu she knew by heart.

"He didn't have that kind of look," Hannah advised. "More like he was thinking about a *woman.*"

"Maybe his ex-wife is giving him trouble."

"Well, if she is, I'd say she's not going to be his ex much longer," Hannah speculated with another chuckle. "That Brad still has a devil of a smile. If I wasn't old enough to be his mother, I'd do a little flirting myself."

"There is no way Brad and Karen are getting back together," Brenda said. "They're worlds apart."

"They had a son together," Jillian said, realizing she couldn't ignore the conversation forever.

"Yes, but that's about all. Believe me, he doesn't care a thing about her—at least, not *that* way."

"Well, it's none of my business," Jillian said.

"Since he was probably thinking of you, you dodo, I think this is your business."

"You're guessing. He might have been thinking of the new librarian. Mandy Thompson is attractive."

Hannah snorted, then broke eye contact and reached into her apron pocket. "I know where that man was staring, and I also know that Mandy Thompson doesn't own a pet store across the town square," she announced as casually as if she'd said, "Do you want fries with that?"

Brenda chuckled. Jillian folded her menu, knowing she was beat.

Hannah poised a well-worn pencil above her trademark small green pad. "You two want the usual?"

"Sure," Brenda said, handing Hannah her unread menu. "Do you have cornbread today?"

"You bet I do. I'll have that out in a jiffy."

Hannah went back to the counter and Brenda again turned her attention to Jillian. "So, what's really going on? I promise not to tell Brad anything if you don't want me to."

"I don't want you two talking about me at all. I don't know why neither one of you listen to me! I swear, it's genetic. You two are as gossipy as Greta and Millicent."

"Oh, we're not that bad. Brad doesn't gossip at all. He just asked about *you.*"

"Sounds like gossip to me."

"Sounds like sincere interest to me. I think it's terribly romantic."

"I think it's just terrible. Let's talk about something else."

"Jillian, you are no fun at all!"

"I'm just a little more mature than you two. You're the worse, but Brad is almost as bad. I think you're stuck at about age fifteen."

"That's mean, Jillian. I'm a responsible, married woman with a daughter of her own. I'm not *fifteen.*"

"Okay, not usually. But about this one subject, you are definitely a teenager."

"You're not going to tell me how you feel about him, are you?"

"Absolutely not. The only other person that I would be more reluctant to tell how I feel is him."

"I knew it! You're crazy about him!"

"How do you come up with these leaps in logic? No, I am not crazy about him."

"If you didn't care, or if you were still mad at him, you wouldn't have any problem voicing your opinion. I know you, Jillian. You're crazy about him."

"I am not!"

"Are to," Brenda declared with a grin, truly resembling the fifteen year old Jillian had accused her of mimicking.

Thankfully, Hannah brought their order before anymore verbal debate could continue. Brenda smiled slyly throughout lunch, as if she'd just found out that the head cheerleader had sex with the quarterback on the fifty yard line after the homecoming game. Jillian tried to ignore her friend's obsession, despite the fact she'd give anything to know what questions Brad had asked about her.

Anything except her pride, she mentally amended. She wasn't about to admit that she was responding to Brad's return in just a slightly more mature manner than the Patterson twins.

On Saturday after they'd taken the puppies home—just five days after *the kiss*—Jillian looked up from her counter as the bell over the door jangled, a smile on her face, and realized that she was waiting for Brad to show up.

The thought frightened her.

She spent the next fifteen minutes discussing hairballs with a older man who'd adopted a long-haired cat from the shelter in Tyler. After explaining the remedies, showing him how to brush a feline, and making him promise to bring his pet into the store soon, she was again left alone.

And thinking about Brad.

With a frustration she rarely experienced, about twenty minutes before closing time she tore into the small animal enclosures, changing cedar bedding, cleaning the glass sides where little fingers had left countless smudges since yesterday. The guinea pigs protested in the high-pitched, squealing voices that had earned them the misnomer "pig." They ran from plastic logs to fake rock "houses" as Jillian wiped the large enclosure, set on a pedestal so children could look inside and she could easily reach the critters.

The second pen contained much quieter but easily excitable hamsters. They'd apparently held a wild pool party, spilling water and food into the bedding. Jillian rolled up the sleeves of her embroidered denim shirt and went to work, deciding a thorough cleaning was best. She placed the hamsters in a smaller wire cage, then scooped all the damp and soiled cedar shavings into a plastic bag. The dust and allergens made her sneeze. Hands deep in hamster mess, she rubbed her itchy nose on her sleeve, smearing the lip gloss she'd applied earlier—just in case.

Just in case Brad Patterson showed up, she added with a twinge of resentment. She didn't want to fix herself up for him. She didn't want to care if he came by every afternoon. However, she didn't seem to be able to stop herself. The realization that she'd quickly fallen under his charm once again made her teeth grind.

Darn him for moving back to Scottsville when he'd built a perfectly good life in Houston. Thousands of bright, talented children lived in big cities. Jeremy didn't have to grow up in this small town. Maybe she should point out that Scottsville lacked many of the amenities older kids expected, like video arcades, amusement parks, and malls.

Tired and out of sorts, she carried the plastic bag to the trash out back, then returned to the small storage room for clean cedar shavings. She had to move a ripped bag of charcoal to get to the bedding material. Her hands came away blackened, she realized in disgust. She was a mess!

Her unruly curls had escaped the scrunchy holder, falling into her eyes, getting stuck on what little remained of her lip gloss. She pushed the curls away, realizing at the last second that she'd smeared charcoal from her mouth to her cheek. Great. Now she probably looked like one of those warring Scottish Highlanders in that Mel Gibson flick.

Well, she might as well finish up. Few customers came in late in the afternoon on Saturday. Unlike her, most people had a *life.* They went to Tyler or Longview to the movies or dinner, or they spent time with friends at home.

Brad probably had a date tonight, she speculated as she poured cedar shavings into the hamster pen, sneezing again, knowing that her nose was now as red as a beet. Maybe he'd met the librarian and asked her out. Maybe he'd met another woman, a stranger or an old friend who welcomed him with open arms.

Jillian had no idea why she'd let herself believe he was serious about *her.* During this week he'd been friendly but hardly romantic. In fact, he'd been the perfect dad, treating her in a very gender-neutral way that she'd initially appreciated.

She didn't want to explore why she'd suddenly determined

his lack of interest was bad—at the same time she'd imagined him partying with some hot date.

Hadn't she told herself time and again that he'd grow bored with Scottsville? Hadn't she warned herself not to get involved with him? She was the biggest fool ever to stroll around the town square, she decided as she returned the nearly empty bag of bedding to the storage room. She pushed her hair out of eyes with the sleeve of her other arm, then reached toward the light switch. Next time she saw Brad Patterson, she was going to tell him—

"You're a mess."

His amused voice stopped her like a cattle prod to the chest. Her mouth opened, her hand dangled limply near the light switch, and her lungs forgot to take in air. She blinked, not sure he was really there . . . but he was. Leaning against the doorway of her storage room, dressed in gray slacks and a fisherman's sweater that emphasized his wide shoulders, he indeed looked as though he was on a date.

Jillian peered around him, expecting to see a buxom blonde or a petite brunette hanging onto his arm.

"What are you doing?" he asked in the same tone of voice.

"Nothing!" she said, straightening, pushing back more of her wayward hair with one finger. "I just thought I heard something."

"Probably some of your restless menagerie. I'm the only person here."

"I was just getting ready to close. I didn't expect any more customers."

"Obviously," he said, his voice and eyes full of humor—at her expense. "I meant, what have you been doing to get so dirty?"

"I'm cleaning out the hamster cage," she said, drawing herself up as tall as possible, tucking her hands close to her sides. "Some of us do manual labor, you know."

"Don't try to pick a fight with me, Jillian. I'm in too good a mood."

She didn't want to ask him why, but obviously didn't keep her curiosity out of her expression.

"I'll tell you why," he said, continuing as if she'd asked the question. "Brenda is keeping Jeremy tonight, I found a great antique trunk this afternoon in Gladewater, and I have plans to ask someone out for dinner."

"I knew it! I knew you were going out tonight," she said with bitter satisfaction, trying to brush by him in the narrow doorway.

"I'd hoped *we* would be going out tonight," he said, his blue-gray eyes dancing with humor as he lightly caught her arm.

"We?" she responded weakly.

"Yes, as in you and me. Or, if you're one of those grammatically challenged television personalities, you and I."

She must have looked pretty stunned. Or maybe poleaxed would be a better description, because he burst out laughing.

"Brad Patterson, this is not funny."

"You should be standing here, then, looking through my eyes. You're an amusing sight."

"Don't you dare laugh at me!"

"Or you'll what?" he said, mimicking a familiar childhood dare, leaning closer.

She wanted to stamp her foot. She wanted to smear charcoal all over his grinning face. Maybe just one little streak . . .

"Don't even think about it," he warned, grasping her wrist as she raised her right hand. "I think a better option is for you to get cleaned up."

"I was just on my way to do that when I got waylaid by a laughing hyena."

"Tsk, tsk. And I was so sure I was going to pleasantly surprise you."

"Your surprises haven't been real successful so far," Jillian pointed out. "I'm still getting over your move back home."

"No you're not. You're glad I'm here."

"Brad Patterson, you are the most conceited man who ever lived!" She pulled away from his light grasp and planned to walk on by. He obviously didn't have the same idea.

"We've had this discussion before," he said, slipping up behind her. When she kept on walking, he ran his large, warm hands from her shoulders down her upper arms and stopped her—mostly from surprise. Then he leaned so close that his minty breath teased her neck and jaw, and his body heat scorched her back. "I'm confident, Jilly. Isn't that one of the things you always . . . liked about me?"

"I don't remember," she lied, closing her eyes against the memories of his surprise embraces. Warm hands, a lean, eager body pressed close. Firm lips and a tongue that could melt her skin like chocolate on a summer day. Oh, she remembered, all right. He'd pull her into a hallway, or jump out from behind a tree. She'd turn in his arms, her lips parted and ready . . . .

"I think you do," he whispered, his mouth so close to the sensitive skin beneath her ear that she wanted to groan in frustration as his hot, moist breath caressed her.

If she turned in his arms right now, his beautiful sweater would be filthy from charcoal smears and cedar shavings. She could get him good for making her think he wasn't showing up—and that he had a date tonight.

But, she realized with a deflating sigh, she couldn't punish him for her own wishes and doubts. He hadn't said he'd stop by the store. He didn't owe her any explanations about his social life.

On the other hand, how dare he assume she'd be alone tonight?

"What made you think I'd be around tonight? I might have had a hot date," she said with as much bravado as she could muster with him standing so close.

"Simple—I asked Brenda."

"Oh." Brenda, gossip extraordinare, had come through again. Jillian was really going to have to talk to her best friend again—not that it would do any good!

"I thought we might go into Longview for dinner," he said, turning her around as easily as a trainer handled a show poodle. "Do you remember all the times we went to Johnny Cayce's with my folks? Dad loved the fried shrimp and Mom always checked out the plate collection on the walls."

"And we would play Ms. Pacman in the hallway by the restrooms."

"Sometimes. We also used to slip outside while my parents had coffee and pie."

"Do you think they knew we were making out behind the restaurant?"

"Of course they did. You have no idea how swollen your lips were or how pink your cheeks got," he said with a grin.

"Oh, thanks! Now I have something else to be embarrassed about when I see them again."

"There's no need to be embarrassed. It's not like we were having a quickie in the back seat of the Buick."

"Brad!"

"Well, I'm just pointing out that we behaved like typical teenagers who'd been dating for a long time. Mom and Dad knew how we felt about each other. They were young once themselves."

"I know, but—"

"No 'buts.' Why don't you get cleaned up and we'll check out Johnny Cayce's? I'd like to see how much it's changed."

"Changed?" she scoffed, smiling despite Brad's super-confident assumption that she wanted to go out to dinner with him. "The restaurant hasn't changed at all. In fact, the Ms. Pacman game is still in the hall."

"You're kidding!" he said with a grin. "Now we have to go. I challenge you to best two out of three."

"Loser buys dinner?"

"Of course."

"Good. That gives me all the more incentive to beat your socks off."

Brad's laughter followed her around the store as she locked the front door, returned the hamsters to their enclosure, and turned off the overhead lights. Soon only the soft glow of the aquariums in the rear and the heat lamps for the lizards illuminated the store.

"I'm going upstairs to clean up now. You can stay down here or you can come into my living room. But I warn you," she said with a shake of her finger, "no comments on my unfolded laundry or the unfinished puzzle."

"I wouldn't think of it," he claimed innocently.

"Okay, then. You can come up."

"I knew I'd get lucky tonight," he said in a mock-leering tone as they headed for the steps.

"Nope. Not even making out behind the bushes," she answered as she climbed the steps. Cleo darted around her feet in a mad dash upstairs.

"No quickie in a Buick?"

"Not even a Buick. Definitely not a pick up truck."

They both laughed. Suddenly the tension lifted, and Jillian felt young again. And comfortable—with Brad and with their renewed relationship. They still hadn't talked about the past, but maybe that was for the best. Perhaps starting over was the right thing to do. Or at least exploring the possibility of starting over. She was tired of making assumptions. From now on, she vowed, she'd take one day at a time.

She motioned for him to make himself at home, then retreated to the bathroom. After gasping at her reflection in the mirror, she had to admit she really was a mess. By all rights, Brad should have run screaming out the door.

He hadn't, though. He'd seen her with a red nose before. He'd seen her dirty, bruised, and scratched. He'd seen her dressed to the nines for the prom, too.

Today—or tonight, she amended—they'd have their first official date as mature adults. Nice and easy, one step at a time.

So why were butterflies fluttering around inside her stomach? And why couldn't she scrub that silly grin off her face?

Chapter Six

Brad smiled all the way to Longview. Thirty miles of companionable silence in his truck, broken only by his comment over a new business that had started since he'd left, or an old one that had gone broke. Of course, they couldn't see much as twilight turned to darkness. He flipped on the radio, finding a song that they'd listened to in the eighties. The music seemed to open a door, and they shared some memories along the way. He could tell that Jillian had relaxed by the time they pulled off of Highway 80 into the restaurant parking lot.

The large bushes where they'd made-out as teenagers were still back there, only they'd grown even higher. He raised one eyebrow and gave Jillian a leering grin, which made her laugh.

The sound swelled in his heart until he wanted to take her in his arms and pretend eleven years hadn't passed.

But, of course, they had. Jeremy's existence proved that years had gone by. Jillian had a successful business she seemed to love—even when she cleaned out the cages. They'd both changed in subtle ways. Brenda claimed Jillian had grown more stubborn as she'd matured, and Brad could see that to some degree. He'd always known and admired Jillian's strong will, so he wasn't surprised.

He wanted to know if she was truly happy. If owning and running the pet store fulfilled her dreams. After all, she'd wanted to become a vet as much as he'd wanted to pursue computer science. Had her father's accident taken away her dream of going to college, or had the tragedy given her more options? He needed to understand, but like many other aspects of their relationship, he sensed that if he pushed her for answers, she'd push him away. He wasn't willing to sacrifice their second chance at happiness just to appease his curiosity.

Dinner went as well as the drive to Longview. Some of the waitresses at Johnny Cayce's were the same ladies who had served them dinner many years ago. One remembered him and asked about "the folks." He explained that his parents had retired to South Texas a few years ago. When she asked how long he and Jillian had been married, an awkward moment followed. Fortunately, another waitress brought their salads, saving him from providing a long-winded explanation that was bound to push some hot buttons with Jillian.

As they dug into their food, the incident forgotten, Brad felt more and more like he and Jillian had slipped into a time warp. At the end of the meal, however, there were no parents to escape, no chaperones to stop them from saying or doing whatever they wanted.

No one except themselves—and a four year old waiting at Brenda's house. Nothing except that pesky problem from their past—the fact he'd gone off to college alone, then broken up with her.

Sooner or later, he thought as they left the parking lot for the drive back to Scottsville, they were going to have to talk about what had happened. Not shout, not accuse, not defend. Just talk, as two rational adults. One of the problems with that scenario was that they were rarely alone. Usually Jeremy accompanied him to the pet store, or, if Jillian came over, Jeremy was there. The two times they'd been alone together had made her nervous and jumpy. Brad supposed she felt safe with a four-year-old chaperone, but he wanted more than stolen moments saying goodnight, or a surprise encounter at the pet store. He wanted them to spend time together so they could work out these issues—and move on to the next stage of their relationship.

Which led him to the second point: He had a feeling Jillian didn't share his enthusiasm for moving forward. She felt safer keeping their relationship "friendly" and not bringing up the past. But they could only walk that tightrope for so long. Soon, he hoped, she'd see that they needed to get beyond their pasts and go forward into the future.

He must have sighed, because she turned to him and said, "You're awfully quiet. Is something wrong?"

"Not really. I was just thinking about what a good time I had tonight. We should do this more often."

She fell silent for several long moments, during which his stomach clenched into a tight fist.

"You mean like a date?"

"Yes, I mean like dating. You and me, going out. Getting to know each other again." He tried to keep his tone light, even as he knew she'd rebel against such an open approach.

"I don't think that's a good idea," she answered in a soft voice, looking down at her hands.

He wanted to pull the car over to the side of the road, grab her by the shoulders, and kiss her senseless. He didn't, of course. The easiest way to make Jillian even more stubborn was to try to bully her. That hadn't worked when she was ten, and he knew it wouldn't work with her now, at twenty-eight.

"Can you tell me why we shouldn't try?" he asked as reasonably as possible.

"Can you tell me why we should?"

He thought about his answer as he passed a van pulling into a gas station. Then they were alone, his truck's headlights piercing the darkness of a road that, before the interstate, had been a major highway through Texas.

"I don't think either one of us would be happy if we didn't

try, Jillian. There's still a spark between us. I know you've felt it too. Why let the past ruin what may be our chance at happiness now?''

"Why delude ourselves into thinking we can let go of the past?''

"I'm willing to let go if you are," he offered.

"That's easy for you to say, Brad. You weren't the one left behind. I didn't ask you if I could go out with other people. I didn't tell you what a marvelous time I was having while you weren't there!''

Her voice rose as anger spurred her on. He pulled off the highway into a deserted diner's parking lot, releasing his seat belt with a jerk.

"Then let's talk about what happened. Let's get it all out in the open. Maybe then we can move on.''

"There's no need. We both know what happened.''

"Do we? I'm not sure we totally understand the other side.''

"I know what you said, what you did. I know how excited you were to go to college on that scholarship. I didn't want to stop you, Brad, but I couldn't go with you. Let's just leave it at that, okay?''

"No, I don't think we should leave it at that. There's a lot you're leaving out, Jillian, like your father's accident.''

"That's something neither one of us had any control over. I don't see how discussing what happened to him will make any difference.''

"I think it would.''

She shook her head. Brad wanted to scream in frustration. Instead, he took a deep, calming breath. "All right, if you don't want to talk about the past, let's talk about the present—and the future. Can you honestly say that you aren't attracted to me?''

"There goes your conceit kicking in," she said, although without the anger she'd given off just moments ago.

"Not conceit, just reality. I'm perfectly willing to admit I'm attracted to you. I'm also willing to speculate that you know how much you affect me.''

"Your hormones are not my problem, Brad Patterson," she said in a huff.

He leaned closer. "At seventeen and eighteen, I might have

been influenced by hormones. At thirty, what I'm feeling is something else.''

That confession brought on total silence from the passenger seat. He knew she wouldn't ask him "what else." Finally, she said, ''Maybe you think you're attracted to me because I'm off limits.''

''You think so?'' he asked, leaning closer, winding a curly strand of her red hair around his finger.

''That's one explanation,'' she said in a throaty voice, just above a whisper.

''I don't think you're as off limits as you'd like me to believe, Jillian Snow. I don't think you're cold and icy at all.'' His lips brushed her cheek as he inhaled her special fragrance. Fresh, clean, a hint of raspberries, a touch of cool night air. Her warmth drew him closer, until his lips rested beside her ear and her curls enveloped him.

''Tell me you don't feel this, too. Tell me what we're both feeling isn't real,'' he whispered.

Her hand slid to his shoulder as a tremor shook her body. With a sigh, she turned her head. In the darkness her lips found his, opened, flowed together with a rush of sensation that made him spin out of control. He deepened the kiss, slanted his lips across hers, claimed her mouth with his tongue. She kissed him back, just like the girl he'd known, like the woman she'd become in his arms.

They broke for air, but only for a moment. She sought his mouth once again, pressing herself closer until their chests met. His hand slipped beneath her jacket until he found her breast, covered with a sweater that couldn't hide the hardened nipple from his searching fingers.

She moaned into his mouth and he kissed her harder, his ears roaring with the knowledge that they were meant to be together like this. That nothing had ever felt so right. She was the woman for him. She'd always been the one. He'd just been too stupid, too immature, to see.

Her hand slipped beneath his jacket and kneaded his back, urging him closer. He wondered insanely if they could make love in the small rear seat of an extended cab pickup truck. He was perfectly willing to try ...

Lights penetrated his closed lids, then the roar of a passing car and a long blast of a horn brought him back to Earth. Brad suddenly realized they were clearly visible from the road, easily identifiable in his big red truck.

Jillian broke away with a gasp, her eyes wide, her lips swollen and parted. Her breathing heavy, she pushed back her tousled hair, then touched her cheeks.

"I can't believe we did that," she said in a breathless, throaty voice that nearly sent him into the passenger seat again.

"I can," he admitted, his own voice unsteady. "And it's going to happen again, Jillian, because we *are* attracted to each other—physically as well as emotionally."

He could tell she wanted to deny his claim. Her head was poised to shake back and forth. But then she deflated like a balloon, her eyes breaking contact with him. "Maybe," she said softly. "So, what are we going to do about this?"

"I think some more dates would be the answer. I mean, I don't expect you to jump right into my bed or anything, although that would be a nice possibility too." He kept his tone as light as he could, given the fact he wasn't joking. Having her in his bed *tonight* seemed like a real good idea at the moment.

"You want me to forget about the past and just go on from here?"

He hesitated before answering. "I think that at some time we have to talk about what happened eleven years ago. But I also believe that we should pursue our relationship now. I don't think those two things are mutually exclusive."

"I don't know if I can do that, Brad."

"Why don't you try?" He leaned forward and smoothed the hair away from her face with a sweep of his hand. "As a matter of fact, I dare you," he added with a grin.

A sparkle lit her eye, then she slowly smiled. "You're on, Patterson."

Okay, this dating business was going pretty well, Jillian thought two weeks later as she, Brad, and Jeremy drove back from Tyler. She always closed the store on Sunday, and they'd decided to take Jeremy to a new pizza place in lieu of a family dinner. Her dad had a standing invitation with friends from church, and Brenda couldn't have been happier to "excuse" them from dinner at her house. The darn matchmaker had a gleam in her eye every time Jillian mentioned something she and Brad had done together.

"So, Jeremy, do you like your new clothes?" They'd stopped by the mall after lunch to do a little shopping since Brad claimed Jeremy grew an inch a month.

"Yeah," he said distractedly, playing with a hand-held computer game Brad had bought him at the toy store on the way out.

"'Yes, Miss Jillian,' is a better answer, son," Brad advised in a fatherly tone, glancing into the rearview mirror for a look at his good, if somewhat less formal, offspring.

"Yes, Miss Jillian," Jeremy mimicked in a tone only a child could produce.

Brad shook his head. "I don't think I'm impressing him with much respect for his elders."

"I think that's a rather hard concept for a four year old," Jillian said. "I know from the kids who come into the store. I'm just thankful if they have any restraint in handling the animals or my supplies." She shifted in her seat to get a better look at Brad. "I think you're doing a great job with Jeremy."

He glanced at her briefly before returning his attention to the road. "You do? Why, I think that's the first nice thing you've said about me, Miss Jillian," he teased in an exaggerated Southern drawl.

She laughed. "Surely not the first. But I'm serious. Jeremy is a good kid. I can see from the way he treats the puppies. He's pretty mature for four."

"I'm almost five," he chipped in from the backseat. "Aunt Brenda says my birthday is comin' up soon. When is that, Daddy?"

"March twelfth. Yes, that's less than two weeks away. Are you excited?"

"Yes!" Jeremy answered with more animation. "Do you know what I want for my birthday?"

"I think so," Brad replied, amusement in his voice. "He's only told me about twenty times," he whispered to Jillian.

She smiled, remembering how exciting birthdays were for a child. Brad and Brenda already had theirs for the year back in January. Jillian wasn't looking forward to her next one in

September. Twenty-nine seemed so final . . . her last year before the big three-oh.

"Is Mommy coming to my birthday party?" Jeremy suddenly asked, jolting Jillian back to reality.

"No, but you're going to visit her in Houston the weekend after your birthday. She'll have your presents and cake there."

"Why can't she come to my party in our new town?"

"Because . . . because she's working in Houston, Jeremy," Brad explained with patience, although Jillian could tell the subject wasn't one he cared to discuss. "She's looking forward to you visiting her at her place."

"Are you coming to Houston, Daddy?"

"No, I'm not. Your mother is picking you up."

"Oh."

The back seat fell silent. Jillian heard the beeps and whooshing noises made by the computer game. Otherwise, the interior seemed ominously silent.

"We can talk about her later, if you want," Brad said in a low voice for Jillian's ears only.

"No, that's okay. It doesn't bother me at all," she said in a tone meant to convince Brad that the fact he'd been married was of no concern. "I'm just glad you get along well enough to share Jeremy so easily."

"So far, so good, although who knows what the future holds."

"What does that mean?"

"Nothing, much. I just get this feeling sometimes that she might want custody. She wasn't real happy that I moved away from Houston after the divorce, although she didn't protest my custody of Jeremy at the time we split up."

"I take it she's still really into her career, then."

"Yes, she is. I liked that about her when we first met. She was so focused on what she wanted, so sure that she'd get it."

"I can see how that would be attractive to you," Jillian said, hoping she didn't sound too critical.

"What do you mean?"

"Just that you have the same quality. You knew what you wanted and went after it."

He thought about that for a moment, maneuvering in the traffic to get on Interstate 20. Jeremy's computer game contin-

ued to beep and whirl in the back, telling Jillian that he wasn't
paying any attention to the adults' conversation.

"I knew what kind of career I wanted. That's a little different
than wanting success above all else."

"Is that what she did?" Jillian asked before thinking. "Sorry,
forget I asked. I'm sticking my nose in again."

"No, that's okay. I don't mind talking about Karen, as long
as I'm careful what I say in front of him," Brad said, nodding
his head toward the back.

"We can talk later," Jillian offered.

"There's not much to say, really. She wanted to become a
successful attorney in a town full of potentially successful
lawyers. I wasn't as driven, I suppose, to be the top computer
guru who ever lived. Jeremy was . . . Well, let's just say that
I was crazy about being a father from the first moment I saw
him."

And she wasn't crazy about being a mother. The idea went
unsaid as they drove toward Scottsville, but Brad gave Jillian
a brief, piercing look that told her everything he couldn't voice
in front of his son.

She'd always known that Brad was a good father. Brenda
had told her time and again what a responsible person he'd
become. Now Jillian began to understand why he'd come back
to Scottsville, but that didn't answer the question of whether
he would stay. After all, he'd shown his ex-wife and his son
that he was "Super Dad." He'd jumped in with both feet,
buying a traditional house in his hometown, furnishing it with
antiques and homey furniture. He even worked at home so he
could spend more time with Jeremy. The man could be a poster
boy for excellent parenting!

But what about Brad, the man? Jillian wondered. When
would that side of him come out, rebelling against the perfect
father role? Or was this a role? She really didn't know if a guy
could shut down the rest of his life and become the ideal father.

All she knew was that women had a hard time with balancing
the role of wife, mother, and lover. Brad didn't have the role
of husband any longer, but surely he wasn't planning on becoming a monk—not with the way he'd kissed her! And he'd
invited her to his bed, even if he was just joking. Or at least

she assumed he was joking. He remained difficult to read at times, especially as this new, more responsible Brad.

Or maybe he could balance everything. Maybe dating her, being Jeremy's dad, and running his business were all parts of his life that he could juggle with no problems. If so, she wanted to discover his secret formula. The potential to make a fortune with that bit of information was overwhelming!

Jillian didn't have long to wait. After Jeremy's birthday party at Brenda's house, he pulled her into the empty laundry room and shut the door.

"What are you doing?" she asked, laughing at his James Bond approach to getting her alone.

"I wanted to talk to you without five or six children hanging on to your skirt."

"That's an exaggeration and you know it. Besides, I can't help it if the pet store owner is a favorite with kids," she said with a smile.

"You're a favorite with me, too," he said, looping his arms around her waist and drawing her close.

She rested her hands on his shoulders, feeling warm and a little wicked for hiding in Brenda's laundry room with a man who could kiss her socks off.

Despite the glaring overhead light and the distinct aroma of detergent, kiss her he did, pushing her back against the dryer, pressing against her until she knew exactly how naughty his own thoughts were. His mouth slanted and coaxed; their tongues danced in harmony as if they'd been kissing for a hundred years. Her fingers ran through his thick, dark hair and he cupped her bottom, pulling her closer.

"Damn, Patterson," she gasped when they came up for air, "you can pull me into the laundry room anytime if you're going to give me that sort of surprise."

"That's not the surprise," he said, his forehead resting against hers, his breathing ragged. "There's something I wanted to ask you."

Oh, no. Not yet. Not now. She wasn't ready for this. She wasn't sure when she'd be ready for this. She pushed against his shoulders. "Brad, no, I don't think—"

''Don't get all defensive,'' he said, pulling back to look at her. ''Hey, I'm just trying to ask you a simple question. Nothing complicated, okay?''

''What kind of a simple question?'' she asked cautiously.

He pulled a folder from the inside pocket of his sport's coat. ''I have here two tickets, Houston to New Orleans, and reservations at a very nice hotel in the French Quarter. Would you do me the honor of running off with me for the weekend?''

She stared at him, at the folder bearing the name of a Houston travel agency, and wanted to grab the tickets with both hands and tear them in two. ''You want me to run off with you for the weekend, just like that?'' she asked, snapping her fingers in front of his nose. ''Are you crazy? I have a pet store to run! I have responsibilities! I can't just run off to New Orleans because Jeremy is going to be away this weekend.''

''You're turning red,'' he said, taking a step back. ''Take a deep breath.''

''Don't patronize me, you . . . you . . . What were you thinking? How could you possibly believe I could run off with you for the weekend.''

He put up his hands in a defensive posture. ''Look, we need to spend some time together as adults. We've dated, we've taken Jeremy places, we've had dinner with Brenda and Sam. I'm ready to move on. I thought you were too.''

''Move on? Is that the new phrase for 'getting in her pants?' ''

''No! Look, I thought you'd enjoy a weekend away from town. Brenda said you hadn't been on a vacation in over a year.''

''Now Brenda is in on this!''

''She didn't know anything about my plans. I got to thinking about it when I realized Jeremy was going to visit his mother, and that we'd have that time alone.''

''So without checking with me, you made reservations.''

''I wanted to surprise you.''

''Well,'' she said, reaching for the doorknob, ''I'm definitely surprised.''

''Jillian, wait,'' he said, pressing his palm against the door. ''Let's talk about this.''

''Brad, you have absolutely the worst sense of timing. You

always want to talk when it's best to shut up, and you want action when we should have talked. Now let go of this door.''

"Aren't you going to listen to anything I say?"

"No! I'm through listening. I suppose I was right all along, Brad Patterson. You miss the excitement of a big city, and you miss the kind of people who are footloose and fancy free. That's not the way life is in a small town. That's probably why you left and never came back. Fine. I'm glad I found out now, before this . . . we . . . went any further.''

"You're making a leap in logic based on some very wrong assumptions," he warned in a voice suddenly cool and biting.

"I'll tell you what I'm doing. I'm leaping right out this door. I'm leaping right out of your life. Go find someone else to take to New Orleans, Brad, because I'm afraid I'm just not convenient any longer!''

He dropped his hand and she jerked open the door, leaving the laundry room in such haste that she almost ran into Brenda as they both turned the corner into the kitchen.

"What's wrong?" Brenda asked, placing a steadying hand on Jillian's shoulder, concern written all over her face.

"Nothing," she answered, realizing for the first time that tears streamed down her face. She was probably as red as a beet, too. "Everything," she amended.

"Sweetie, what happened? Did you and Brad—"

Jillian heard the door to the laundry room open and her eyes jerked toward the sound. Brad stood in the doorway, his face masked against any emotion.

"Never mind, Brenda," she said, straightening, wiping away the moisture. "I have to go. I was right all along. You should have listened to me. This was *not* a good idea.''

With those last words, she grabbed her purse from the breakfast bar and bolted out the back door. She wasn't sure how she would manage it in a town this small, she vowed as she fumbled for her car keys, but somehow, she was going to avoid Brad Patterson as though he carried the plague.

Chapter Seven

He *was* going to have a good time in New Orleans, Brad told himself Friday afternoon as he kissed Jeremy good-bye at Karen's condo in Houston. Bourbon Street, watch out, he silently vowed as he whipped the truck toward Hobby airport. New Orleans' tourists certainly included a large number of single women. And who said he needed a female companion to have a good time? He'd party with the best of them. Other entertainments awaited him, like good music. Yes, he liked jazz. And then there was . . .

He couldn't think of anything else. With a jerk to the wheel, he steered past a shuttle bus into terminal parking, too impatient to get on with his long weekend to park in the outlying lot. Yes, he was ready to get to New Orleans and have a damn good time.

Jillian was going to miss a great weekend. She'd be sorry she didn't go with him when he got back, relaxed yet exhausted from partying in the French Quarter.

Of course, he wouldn't be able to tell her. She didn't want to talk to him. Brenda had told him that much . . . along with other choice pieces of sisterly wisdom. She'd called him a damn fool, an idiot when it came to women, and a lot of other things. Brenda didn't know everything, though. She didn't understand how he and Jillian needed time alone, as two adults, to get to know each other again.

Hell, for the *first* time—since they'd been teenagers when they were together before. They'd thought they were mature, but obviously weren't. He had to believe that if they'd been more sure of themselves, more confident of their love, they wouldn't have broken up. He would have been more understanding about her father's accident and her need to stay in Scottsville, and she would have been more supportive of his first year at college and all the experiences so new to a young man from East Texas.

But they couldn't relive the past. They could have moved beyond the pain and suspicions, though, if she'd only given them a chance. He'd tried, by showing her the attraction was still there, by sweet dates and family time, by proving he was more mature and settled now than when he graduated from high school. Apparently Jillian wasn't interested in learning more about him. She only wanted to punish him for what had happened.

Well, she was only punishing herself, he thought as he slammed the driver's side door and strode toward the terminal with his carry-on bag. He paused at the monitors, checking the gate for the flight to New Orleans. Great. He had a short walk, then he'd be on the plane and away.

They would have had a great time in New Orleans. Too bad she'd miss it. She could probably use a vacation from her store and all the busybodies in Scottsville who thought they knew what was best for her.

His jaw clenched, he plunked his bag down on the security conveyer and walked through the metal detector. An annoying buzzer stopped him cold. After removing his keys and change, he walked through again, not setting off alarms this time. He grabbed his bag and proceeded to his gate.

Yes, those busybodies were wrecking Jillian's life. Trying to encourage her to get back together with him, they'd only succeeded in making her more skittish. Brenda had warned him that Jillian only got more stubborn when pressed. Besides, they should have left her alone, he thought as he handed his ticket to the airline representative at the gate. If she'd just listened to him, then this whole weekend could have turned out so differently.

"May I help you?" The feminine voice seemed to echo through a thick fog, barely registering as he continued to think about all the advice Jillian was getting from her friends.

If she'd just listened to him . . .

"Sir?"

"What?" Brad said, blinking, seeing the young woman in a crisp blue uniform for the first time.

"Are you boarding this flight?" She reached across the counter. "May I have your ticket please?"

Brad looked down at the envelope in his hand, then back at

the ticket clerk. "No," he said, shaking his head. "No, I'm not boarding this flight."

Jillian leaned over and rested her elbows on the counter while Millicent and Greta argued over whether their parakeets preferred seed with flax or without. The discussion was always the same, but they didn't appreciate either a referee or an expert opinion—until they asked for it. Jillian knew from experience that the two sisters enjoyed talking about their pets almost as much as they enjoyed gossiping about their neighbors.

As she rested her chin in her hands, she wondered if Millicent and Greta talked to their birds about her. She could hear them now . . .

I just know Jillian would have enjoyed going on a trip with that nice Brad Patterson.

You know she wouldn't go away with a young man for a weekend alone. She's not that kind of girl!

I didn't say she was going to stay in his room. I just meant she'd enjoy spending time with him.

She can spend time with him right here in Scottsville.

Only if she has enough flaxseed in her diet.

Jillian jolted upright, blinking at the two sisters. "What?"

Greta smiled at her. "I said we'd like the parakeet food with the flaxseed, dear," she said with a smile. "I think you were daydreaming."

"I hope that's the right one," Millicent said in a worried tone, peering at the bag of bird seed through her lavender-framed bifocals.

"If it's not, you can bring it back," Jillian offered, just as she always did. So far, the sisters had never returned any food. She suspected that the parakeets gladly ate whatever the sisters provided, since they invariably chose top quality products.

As she rang up the sale for the sisters, she could tell they wouldn't be leaving immediately. Both settled their purses on the counter and gazed at her with interest.

"How are things with you, Jillian?" Greta asked.

"Fine. Busy."

"Isn't that little Jeremy just a precious boy? He came to the bakery last week and ordered a special birthday cake,'' Millicent added out of the blue.

"Batman,'' Greta said. "We thought he meant the one from the 1970's television series,'' she added with a chuckle, "but he didn't.''

"That Batman was a wild show, wasn't it? I think that man looked pretty good in his tights, though,'' Millicent said with a sly smile.

"Yes, he did. What was his name? Do you remember, Jillian?'' Greta asked, frowning as she searched her memory.

"No, I'm afraid that was before my time.''

"Really?'' Millicent responded, clearly confused. The dear never realized how old people were. To her, everyone shared common memories. Of course, she was probably already in her fifties during the 1970s, so remarking on Batman's attributes did seem a bit funny.

"Adam West,'' Greta answered her own question with satisfaction.

"His father said he could have any kind of decoration he wanted, but I don't think those comic books are too good for children,'' Millicent said.

"I don't know much about the subject,'' Jillian offered lamely. She didn't have an opinion on children's birthday cakes or entertainment, for that matter. Until recently, she'd had no idea what kids were interested in these days, except for trendy and classic pets. If she remembered correctly, Jeremy's birthday cake had Dalmatians cavorting across the white icing.

She was rather surprised that he hadn't put Beagles on his cake. She also wondered who was taking care of the little dears—aptly named Spot and Whizzer—while Jeremy was visiting his mother—and *his father* was off cavorting like a playboy in New Orleans.

"Here you go, dear.'' Millicent handed her correct change for their purchase.

Well, Jillian thought as she punched in the amount on the cash register, her earlier mood evaporating faster than summer rain on hot asphalt, she hoped he had a terrific time on his little jaunt. She hoped he drank Bourbon Street dry. She hoped he had the world's worst hangover when got on that plane back to Houston. As a matter of fact, she thought as she counted the change into each compartment, for all she cared, he could just stay in Houston. She shut the door with enough force to shake the display of bell-adorned cat collars on the countertop.

"My goodness," Greta said as the tinkling faded away. "Are you all right?"

"I'm fine," Jillian said, struggling to keep her voice even. "I just have a headache."

"Have you tried that new herbal remedy at 'Ye Olde Tea Shoppe?' " Millicent asked.

"No." Jillian rubbed her temples, certain that her head might truly explode if she didn't stop thinking about a certain man. She could tell her face was flushed. Her blood pressure would no doubt soar off the gauge if any medical professional had the bad timing to slap a cuff around her arm right now.

"I think we'd better go," Greta said, looping her hand through Millicent's arm. "Jillian needs some rest."

"That's a good idea, dear," Millicent said, giving Jillian's hand a little pat. "But try that herbal tea. It's wonderful."

"She mixes it with a spot of brandy," Greta whispered over her sister's head.

Jillian smiled despite her burgeoning headache and bad mood.

"I heard that!" Millicent protested as her sister guided her toward the door.

"Ladies, don't forget the bird seed." Jillian grabbed the bag and reached across the counter.

At that moment, the door opened, bringing in a gust of spring-scented wind . . . and the source of all her troubles. Dressed in jeans and a leather jacket, dark hair tousled, legs braced apart, framed by the setting sun, he made quite a picture poised in her doorway. She sucked in a deep breath and tore her eyes away, focusing on her two customers instead.

"Oh, my," Millicent said, placing a hand over her heart in a dramatic pose.

"Hello, young man," Greta said, her eyes giving him a once over. "I thought you were out of town."

"I'm back," he said simply. Jillian had a notion he looked at her when he said that, but she wasn't about to find out.

"I was just closing," she said briskly, straightening the counter.

"Come along, Millicent," Greta said.

Jillian heard the sisters' footsteps. "Nice to see you," Millicent said her sing-song voice as they exited the store.

The door shut with a finality that couldn't be ignored. She looked up, hoping that Brad had gone with the ladies, but, of course, he hadn't.

"Why aren't you in New Orleans?" she asked, staring at him, hoping he understood that she really didn't want to see him, talk to him, or do anything else with him.

He reached over and turned the sign on the door to closed.

"Don't do that!"

"You said you were closing. I'm just trying to help."

"Bull. You're trying to irritate me." She stood behind the register, her hands clenched at her side.

"I think I've already done that," he said walking toward the counter. "What I'm really trying to do is buy us some time together."

"By closing up my store?" She unclenched her fists and crossed her arms over her chest.

"Yes. And by assuming you'd want to go away with me for a weekend."

"Brad, we've already talked about this. I think you should leave."

"No, we haven't talked about this," he said, placing both hands on the counter, leaning forward. His face appeared unreadable, set with unusually grim lines and a furrowed brow. "Jillian, I was wrong. I'm sorry."

She blinked, not sure she'd heard him right. Brad Patterson, apologizing? Her head started to pound with renewed vigor. She took a step backward.

"I'm sorry," he repeated. "I realized at the airport that I didn't want to go to New Orleans."

"Brenda called me and said you'd gone."

He shrugged. "I thought I would go ahead and use the tickets. I thought I'd have a good time—kind of like I was going to show you what you were missing by staying here in Scottsville."

"Why didn't you?" she asked in a soft voice that hardly sounded like her own.

"Because," he said, putting more weight on his arms, leaning farther over the counter, "I knew that New Orleans wouldn't be any fun without you, Jilly. I didn't want to go alone. I didn't want to party by myself or with anyone else.''

''You should have gone.'' Her heart beat faster as she watched his eyes. His clear, blue-gray eyes that more often teased than confessed dark secrets.

''No, I shouldn't have,'' he answered, shaking his head. He pushed away from the counter and walked around the end. ''I only wanted to be with you. At the time I planned the trip, I wasn't thinking of anything besides what *I* wanted, so I never thought about how you'd react to an impulsive weekend away.'' He stopped about two feet away, making no move to come closer or touch her.

Just as well. She wasn't sure how she felt, what she wanted. This new Brad confused her. Why couldn't their relationship be simple? Why did they continue to amaze and frustrate each other?

''Please, say you understand. Say something,'' he asked softly.

''I don't know what to say. I've been so angry with you. All I could think of was that you were so inconsiderate, trying to bend me to your whim. And that you missed your life in a big city, like Scottsville would never be enough for you.''

''I was angry with you too. Angry that you wouldn't give us a chance to be adults together. Angry that you'd dug in your heels because everyone was encouraging you to get back together with me. Angry that I couldn't make you do what I wanted you to do.''

''That's a lot of anger,'' she said, amazed that he'd admitted so much, equally amazed when she realized she'd also poured out her heart.

He nodded slightly. ''Yes, and then I realized that I was doing exactly the same thing to you that all your friends and neighbors were doing.''

''What do you mean?''

''Trying to manipulate you. Trying to influence you.'' He stepped forward, his hands gently holding her shoulders. ''I should have given you more time. I'm sorry,'' he said, his eyes half-hidden as he looked down at her through thick lashes. ''It's not the big city I miss, Jilly. It's you. It's always been you.''

"Damn you, Brad Patterson, for being such a forgivable jerk," she said, trying to sound stern even as her voice clogged with emotions she couldn't name—and didn't care to try. The "old Brad" wouldn't have apologized so sincerely, nor would he have confessed his feelings so freely. She liked this "new Brad" much better. In fact, she was barely able to restrain herself when she wanted nothing more than to throw herself into his arms.

Brad tipped the scales when he pulled her close, tucking her head under his chin. "Let's start over one more time. I'll try not to put any pressure on you, okay?" he asked, punctuating his question with a kiss to her hair. Where his leather jacket parted, she felt his pounding heart, and realized the beat matched her own.

"Okay," she murmured, snuggling closer. "I'll hold you to that promise, Patterson."

"I know you will, Miss Snow," he answered. And she heard the humor in his voice and knew their relationship had been given one more chance to survive . . . and maybe to thrive.

In deference to the great spring weather, Jillian took Saturday afternoon off and drove to Brad's house. She'd packed a simple meal of chicken salad sandwiches, courtesy of Hannah, and lemon cake with cream cheese frosting, courtesy of Millicent and Greta. The only contributions Jillian could claim as her own were plump red grapes and a thermos of iced tea. She wasn't worried about where the food came from, though, because Brad had claimed that anything she brought would be heartily appreciated.

Building a treehouse was hard work.

They'd talked last night after she closed the store, until Brad hid a yawn and claimed he wasn't the least bit sleepy. She realized that he'd put in a long day, driving Jeremy to Houston since he was going there anyway to catch a plane, then driving four hours back to Scottsville.

And then there were the emotions, gallons of feelings, silently trickling from both of them in a steady stream. Jillian had a horrible premonition that if she pulled her finger from the dike, the trickle would turn into a flood. On the other hand, part of her wanted to be washed away in the deluge. She didn't know what to think of these conflicting desires, so she did her best to keep the trickle going, steady and strong.

Last night had not been the time to get washed away in a flood. She and Brad both were too vulnerable. Saying goodnight with a simple, yearning kiss had been the best for both of them.

Or so she told herself as she tossed and turned, craving his warmth, wishing she could feel the steady beat of his heart pressed close to hers. Instead, she'd spent the night with a restless cat and a dripping bathtub faucet.

Today, with daffodils blooming beneath budding maple trees and the town square decorated in pastel eggs and smiling bunnies, she pushed aside thoughts of desire and frustration and concentrated on more pressing issues . . . like how in the world she could "help" Brad build a treehouse for Jeremy.

She parked around back, leaving the windows down to let in the glorious spring weather. Sunlight danced over her as she walked toward the sound of hammering. High above, wedged between two sturdy limbs and the massive trunk of a Live Oak tree, Brad kneeled on a platform.

"Hey, up there!" Jillian called, shielding her eyes as she looked into the sun. "Do you think you made it high enough?"

Brad set his hammer down and leaned over the edge of the fresh-cut lumber. "This is the best place," he explained with a smile. "Besides, the view is great."

"I'm sure the crows say the same thing," Jillian shot back with a laugh.

"I guess I did go overboard," he admitted, "but come on up and see."

Luckily, she'd had the foresight to pull on old jeans and not the flirty, frivolous long skirt she'd been tempted to wear. Climbing the twenty or thirty steps that Brad had pounded into the tree truck would not have been easy in diaphanous cotton gauze.

"What about the picnic basket?" she asked, shading her eyes once again.

"Leave it. We've got work to do before we eat, woman," Brad announced in his version of a cave man directive.

Jillian laughed. "Okay, but not on the ground. The ants and

other creepy crawlies are out in full force. Do you have a rope up there?''

He threw her one over the side, where is dangled and wiggled like a slow moving snake slithering to earth. ''I come prepared.''

She remembered when those words meant something else entirely, and wondered if he might be thinking of the same scenario. Probably, if she knew Brad at all.

She tied the rope around the handle of the basket, then directed Brad to tie off the rope so their lunch dangled above the ground. As soon as she was sure the lemon cake wouldn't be consumed by starving ants, she began the long climb to the treehouse.

Huffing and puffing, she finally grabbed Brad's hand and let him haul her the rest of the way onto the platform.

''Patterson,'' she said, struggling to get her breath, ''do you realize that your son is only five years old?''

''Yes, I just remembered that. I suppose I should have thought about it earlier, hmm?''

''Maybe,'' she said, straightening while keeping a hand on the tree trunk. ''Wow, this is a great view, though.''

''I know. Once I climbed the tree, I couldn't resist.''

''You could really spy on your neighbors from up here.''

''I know. I'm hoping the couple next door put in a pool— or at least a hot tub. That might be pretty entertaining late at night.''

''You're incorrigible! If they turn over a spade of dirt, I'm warning them about you.''

''Spoiler,'' he accused with a grin. She continued to turn, seeing the view from all angles. When her gaze rested on Brad, a warm, tender smile greeted her.

''I'm glad you came, Jillian,'' he said simply.

She swallowed, then smiled in return. ''I'm not a great carpenter.''

''That's not why I asked you and you know it.''

She glanced away, suddenly shy. Sitting high in this old tree made her feel so isolated, even if they were in view of the world. Still, the dimensions of the platform enforced an intimacy she hadn't felt before, not even in his truck when he'd pressed her against the seat and kissed her senseless.

Escaping Brad's often overwhelming presence wouldn't be easy, not with the ground far below. And yet she wondered why she was thinking of running away, when she wanted to be here with all her heart . . . not to mention the rest of her body.

"So, what are you working on now?" she asked, deciding to ignore both her desires and Brad's innuendoes for the moment.

"I thought a railing would be nice."

"Good choice. Is that what the lumber is for?"

"Yes. I've already cut it, but I may need more. I made the platform a little larger than I'd originally planned."

"Why am I not surprised?" she asked with a laugh.

For the next hour, Jillian handed him boards and he assembled a sturdy railing around three sides of the platform, attaching to four corner posts which would support a roof. The fourth side curved around the massive tree trunk and would provide access to the steps. Brad had explained that he'd put a rope hand-hold there for safety.

This simple treehouse for Jeremy was beginning to resemble the home in last summer's movie version of "George of the Jungle." Come to think of it, Brad reminded her of Brendan Fraser—without the long hair and goofy expression so typical of the actor. Of course, he did have a great body . . .

As she sat on the platform, resting her forearms on her bent knees, she wondered if she could talk Brad into wearing a loin cloth.

The vision of him swinging around his backyard, nearly naked and yodeling at the top of his lungs, brought forth a giggle.

"What's so funny?" he asked, poised to drive in a nail on the other side of the treehouse.

"Nothing much," she said, biting her lip to keep from chuckling. "I just remembered something funny from a movie I saw."

"Tell me about the scene that made you laugh—and why you thought of it just now. You've been awfully quiet over there."

"It's nothing, really."

"Come on, Jillian. You don't want me to get bored, do you?"

"How could you get bored when you have so much construction to accomplish? I think this project may keep you busy until Jeremy grows into this treehouse."

"Low blow, Miss Snow."

"You rhymed. That'll cost you," she teased, referring to their childhood tradition of "punishing" an inadvertent rhyme. She'd get to chose a favor and he'd have to do whatever she said. Would this work any better as adults than as children? Somehow, she doubted Brad would cooperate any more easily now.

"What's it going to cost me?" he asked, kneeling down and placing the hammer on the floor of the treehouse. His expression didn't give him away; he seemed perfectly serious about honoring her request.

"I haven't decided yet," she said, "but I'm considering several possibilities."

"Give me a clue."

She shook her head. "Nope."

"Come on, Jilly, or I'll have to make you talk." He started crawling across the wood like a grinning jungle cat.

"Oh, no you don't!" Now would be a good time to have an express exit from the tree. She scooted back against the trunk.

"Yes. I have you at my mercy." He reached out and snagged her ankle.

She shrieked, startling all the birds in the neighborhood.

"My neighbors will think I'm murdering you," he said with a laugh.

"Maybe they'll come and rescue me," she said, trying not to giggle like a child as Brad pulled on her leg.

"No one can rescue you from the clutches of . . . The Mad Hammer Man."

"The Mad Hammer Man?" She began to laugh in earnest. "Is that the best you can come up with?"

With a sudden move, Brad pulled her away from the trunk, then launched himself on top of her. "I'll teach you not to make fun of me, woman!"

She was already laughing hard when he began to tickle her. His seeking fingers made her squirm like an eel. Too bad she wasn't as slippery! Brad had her firmly under his control, and he wasn't shy about pushing his advantage.

"Give?" he asked, a devilish glint in his eyes.

"I give!" she shrieked as his fingers found her ribs again.

They were both breathing hard from all the laughing when he stopped tickling her, braced himself above her, and looked down. And when she stopped squirming and looked up. Suddenly, their position took on another meaning.

If he lowered his chest, he'd be lying atop her. If she angled her head and parted her lips, he could claim her mouth in a fierce kiss.

As if he read her thoughts, he eased downward until he rested on his elbows, braced on either side of her shoulders. His chest barely teased hers, but his hips pressed intimately against her stomach, one leg between hers. She trembled.

"Give?" he whispered, his lips just a breath away.

Instead of answering, she reached up and captured his head, pulling him down for a kiss that sent her reeling. Explosions of light danced across her closed eyelids as she drank in the taste and feel of him. She sank her fingers deeper into his hair as her body surged toward him. Brad surrounded her with his special scent, tinged lightly with sweat and the spring day. His hands slipped beneath her back, bringing them tighter together. She sank into him, wondering how she'd lived so many years without experiencing this magic . . . and how she ever thought she'd find such wonders with anyone but Brad.

They kissed forever, rolling to their sides on the hard boards, then rolling again until Jillian lay sprawled on top. Her fingers sought the buttons on his shirt, pushing the fabric aside with haste to touch his hot skin. His chest heaved with rapid intakes of breath, the muscles tight and sleek against her hands. When had Brad developed such a body? Why hadn't she been there to experience the change?

She was so intent on undressing him that she didn't realize he'd loosened her shirt from her jeans until he tugged the soft cotton over her head. The blessed coolness of spring air sent ripples over her skin. On her back she felt dappled sunlight— and Brad's stroking hands.

He cupped her bottom, pulled her intimately against him. Her nails dug into his chest as she leaned back, closed her eyes, and moaned low in her throat. Brad answered the sound, pressing himself closer, moving against her in a way that made her gasp. She'd waited too long to feel this way, she thought as she answered his gentle motions.

"You are so beautiful," he whispered.

She opened her eyes and looked down at his handsome, drawn face. The expression in his eyes was so intense that she blinked, startled by the emotions she saw there. Did he really feel so strongly for her? Was this an effect of the passion, not the . . . She hesitated to use the word "love" because they hadn't spoken of anything so serious.

But that was the way he looked at her. She eased against his chest, parted her lips, and kissed him as deeply as possible, telling him how she felt without putting voice to her thoughts.

He threaded his fingers through her hair, loosening it from the holder until it spilled around them in curling tendrils. As he broke the kiss, he buried his face in her hair, his breathing ragged. His lips pressed against her neck, nipped lightly, then kissed the sensitive skin below her ear with such passion that a tremor passed from her neck to her toes.

"Jillian, are you sure you want this? Right here, right now?"

Chapter Eight

She floated up from the sensual pool, emerging into the dappled sunlight and Brad's warm gaze. She blinked, her mind trying to focus on where they were, what they were about to do. But she found thinking beyond the moment impossible, concerning herself with such details as their location unimportant. Right now, she could be lying on the tender grass of Town Square Park or on the rough concrete walkway outside her store. She didn't care . . . she didn't want to know.

"Jillian," Brad whispered, "I want to make love to you more than you can imagine, but I want to make sure you aren't just carried away by the passion."

"What's wrong with being carried away?" she said softly, burying her face in his chest, breathing in his scent.

"Regrets," he answered, tipping her chin up so she looked into his eyes. "We should never have regrets between us again."

She closed her eyes, her mind recognizing the truth even as her body cried out for more. More Brad, more passion. She could easily move against his arousal, could tell him that there would be no regrets. But the truth would still be there, waiting for the clear-headed voice of reason.

She rested her chin on his chest and groaned, the sound like that of pain.

"I'm sorry," he said gently, "but one of us had to think before we made love right here in the open, no thought of tomorrow—"

"No protection," she added, her voice muffled.

His chuckle surprised her. Her eyes popped open. He looked at her with a mixture of passion denied and amusement. "So true. I haven't been carrying anything in my pocket 'just in case' since my father explained condoms to me at the age of fifteen."

Jillian smiled in spite of her frustration. "Fifteen, hmm? I suppose that was a pretty old condom by the time we got around to using it."

"Actually, I still have the original in the bottom of my drawer. I figured it might not be any good after two years, so I got some new ones before we . . ."

"Needed one?" she offered.

"Exactly." He smiled and kissed her nose. "However, if you don't get off me—very carefully, of course—I may forget all about my reservations and the fact that we might provide Jeremy with a brother or sister much sooner than I'd anticipated."

Her mouth fell open as she chewed over his words. He'd *anticipated* having another child? With her?

"Come on, Jilly. You're falling down on your job as carpenter's helper," he said, swatting her bottom when she failed to move.

"Ouch," she said automatically, not really feeling the palm

of his hand as much as the implications of the words he'd tossed out so lightly.

She was just about to ask him what he'd meant when he spoke again.

"How about that late lunch/early supper you brought by? I'm starving."

"You're always starving after—" She blushed when she realized what she'd said so casually.

Brad laughed. "Yeah, and we didn't even have an 'after' this time."

"Don't blame me for that. I was going right along with the flow when you so rudely—and correctly, I might add—pointed out my loose morals and lack of foresight."

"I never said anything about your morals."

"Yes, but I'm sure Scottsville would have enthusiastically taken me to task if anyone had seen my bare bottom from their window or the yard below."

"Or my bare bottom," Brad pointed out with a chuckle as he stood up and offered his hand to her. He pulled her to her feet, steadying her when her legs threatened to buckle. "Easy."

"Watch it, Patterson," she warned. "I'm selective, not easy."

Brad's booming laughter echoed through the trees as he reached over the newly-constructed railing and pulled up the picnic basket.

"Of course," she said, one finger on her chin as she critically appraised his backside, "I wouldn't mind seeing your bare bottom at a later date."

Brad almost choked when his laughter turned to a fit of coughing. He fumbled with the rope, nearly dropping the basket, as he recovered his composure. "You're going to pay for that one," he warned with a dangerous, exciting glint in his eye.

After lunch, they settled against the railing and held hands. Brad knew they'd reached another turning point in their relationship, one that he hoped would carry them forward. As long as he didn't screw up again, he silently added. From now on, he'd do whatever necessary to earn Jillian's trust. If that meant they'd wait to make love, so be it. If he had to curb his desire for weeks to show her that he wanted more than a fling, he could do that.

What he wouldn't do was act impulsively, without thinking of her feelings or the consequences. He'd made that mistake earlier, when he'd booked the trip to New Orleans without thinking about her responsibilities.

"How's your father?" Brad asked.

Jillian looked up from a fairly serious contemplation of their clasped hands. "He's fine. He barely walks with a limp anymore."

"He must have had a lot of physical therapy." The last time Brad had seen Herman Snow, the man had been in a hospital bed, heavily medicated for pain, one of his legs crushed and the other one broken in several places.

"He did, for years. Daddy said the cure was nearly as bad as the accident," she said with a distressing little chuckle that told Brad the therapy had been painful for her too.

"I'm sorry I wasn't there for you, Jillian."

She looked up at him, her brows puckered as though she was full of confusing emotions. "I'm sorry you weren't, either. I needed you, Brad. I'd never been through anything like that. I barely remember my mother's illness, although I'm sure her sickness seemed to last forever when I was a child. Daddy's injury was so sudden. When his truck ran off the road and flipped, I thought that was the worst. He was so hurt . . ."

"I know, sweetheart," Brad said, holding tight to her hand.

"But I was so angry when the company said the accident was Daddy's fault, as if he put those retread tires on the truck, as if he made one of them blow on purpose."

"Corporate jerks."

"Darn right. They didn't even admit they blamed the tire company until our lawyer started depositions. And they nearly dared us to sue them! They said we'd be tied up in court forever."

"Typical corporate response," he commiserated.

"We were lucky that the attorney was willing to take the case on a contingency basis, or we'd still be paying off Daddy's surgery and physical therapy bills."

Brad stroked her hand, silently encouraging her to keep talking. He knew she needed to air all the unpleasantness of the past. She needed to admit her anger at everyone—including him—so they could move past the painful memories. "So you finally got a good settlement?"

"Yes, but it took five years. Daddy wanted to quit, but not me. I wanted that company to admit that he hadn't driven that truck recklessly. He wasn't speeding, nor napping, or doing anything that caused the blowout. If he'd had good tires on the truck, he would never have gotten hurt." She paused. "I'm sorry. I hardly ever talk about the accident or what happened afterward. I don't know why you'd want to listen to me rant and rave," she said, looking up through the leaves of the old live oak.

"Maybe because I wasn't there to listen the first time."

She turned to him then, searching his face, his eyes. "You really have changed, haven't you?"

"God, I hope so," he said with a chuckle and a shake of his head. "Who would want to be eighteen forever?"

"According to Brenda, any woman who's had a baby," Jillian joked.

"Okay, maybe, but I doubt it. Eighteen year olds are pretty single minded and stupid, in my opinion."

"Eighteen-year-old boys, you mean," Jillian corrected.

"You're right. You were pretty mature even at seventeen."

"Well, thanks, but I can look back and see that I made mistakes too. Boys might be ruled by their hormones, but girls seem to be overwhelmed by the green monster."

"Jealousy?"

"That's right. I had my share," she confessed.

"Of what?" he encouraged.

"Do you really want to hear this?"

"Yes, I do."

"Well, okay." She looked up at the limbs overhead and squinted as sunlight filtered through, hitting her eyes. "I was jealous that you got to go off to Texas A & M and I didn't. I was jealous of the fun you said you were having, the new friends who spent time with you and the girls you talked to between classes. Pretty much, I was jealous of everything about your life in College Station."

"At the time, I thought you were being . . . Heck, I don't know how to explain what I thought. Maybe I knew you were jealous, but being young, I put the label 'petty' on your feelings. I wasn't able to put myself in your shoes, Jillian, because I'd never faced anything traumatic in my life.''

''I can see that,'' she said, nodding, ''now. I wasn't that clear-headed when I felt myself losing you, after I'd come so close to losing my dad.''

''You shouldn't have been expected to be rational and clear-headed. I should have been the one to remain cool and objective. Instead, I let my own excitement over going off to college, meeting new friends, and just experiencing the world overwhelm my common sense. Or, as I've said before, what little common sense an eighteen year old possesses.''

She sat there silently for a moment, then shifted on the hard wooden platform. ''You said that you were excited over your new life. Is that generally why you wanted to break up? Or was there someone in particular?''

He unlaced their fingers, then placed his arm around her shoulders. ''I didn't want to break up, sweetheart. I thought, in my stupid teenage way, that if you believed we might break up, you might try harder to get involved in my life. I know it sounds lame, but that's all I could think of. I didn't really understand how seriously injured your father was, and I couldn't understand why you didn't share my excitement over college life.''

''That was pretty lame, Patterson,'' she said softly.

''Tell me about it. When you said that you didn't want to see me again, I was too shocked to react. Then when you actually wouldn't talk to me, I was angry—at you, at the whole situation, and then, years later, at me. I think I spent my four years at A & M acting out of anger.'' He squeezed her shoulders. ''So, in a way, you got your revenge on me. I was pretty miserable for years after you dumped me.''

''After I dumped you? Have you been sleeping?'' she asked incredulously, poking him in the ribs with her elbow. ''I thought we'd just agreed that you broke up with me!''

''Well, sort of. But remember that I didn't really mean to break up with you.''

''Oh, right. You were trying to get my attention.''

''Exactly! I'm glad you understand.''

''Brad Patterson, you rat!''

He used the arm around her shoulders to spin her toward him, capturing her off-balance body in an embrace that pulled her across his lap. "I'm glad you're not mad at me anymore, Jilly," he said just inches from her lips. "Now give me a kiss. We've got work to do."

"I don't feel like—"

He cut off her protest with a powerful kiss. She was obviously startled, but she quickly parted her lips and kissed him back. By the time they broke apart, she was laughing and he couldn't hold back a grin.

"Sweetheart, you *feel* great," he admitted, "but don't keep on tempting me. We've got a treehouse to build and only a little more than a day. If you keep on jumping my bones, I'll never get finished."

He kept on laughing, even when she growled ferociously and punched his shoulder.

"I suppose you should know that Brad and I are dating again," Jillian said after sitting down at her dad's table on Sunday after church. As usual, she'd picked him up that morning for services, then planned to eat their meal together. Sometimes he went out with friends later; other times Jillian stayed around the family home, doing small repairs or cooking a special meal for later in the week. Today she was going to visit Brad after lunch.

"I figured you would. Guess all that denyin' you were goin' to get back together was a bunch of bull," he said in his usual blunt manner. Herman Snow didn't believe in "beating around the bush," as he liked to say.

"I meant it at the time," she said in defense, helping herself to a big serving of mashed potatoes.

"I suppose. You two were bound to end up married or in another state. Can't imagine the two of you within two hundred miles and not pressed tighter than a woolly worm on a juicy leaf."

"Dad, we're not talking about the 'm' word, and besides, that's not a very flattering comparison! Am I the woolly worm or the leaf?"

He scoffed at her protest. "You know what I mean."

She shrugged. "I suppose you're right, although Brad *has* been back to town for visits in the past eleven years. He just never came around *me*."

" 'Course not," her dad said in a matter-of-fact tone. "He was a married man. He wouldn't come around."

"I'm glad you think so highly of him. How about me? Do you think I'd fool around with a married man?"

"Of course not. All I'm sayin' is that he was keepin' himself away from temptation."

Like she was the *femme fatale* of Scottsville. Jillian had to chuckle at that image.

"I'm going over after lunch to help him finish a treehouse that was supposed to be for Jeremy. I'm afraid it's too high up, though."

"The boy'll grow into it."

"Yes, but if he fell, he could be seriously hurt."

"You sound like a mother," he said with a sly smile, looking up with a forkful of food poised in mid-air.

"I . . . I was just making a logical comment." She did not sound like a mother . . . did she? She'd never thought of herself in a maternal role. She'd spent so much of her time policing the pet store against grasping little fingers that she didn't usually think of herself as having full-time responsibilities for a child. Besides, having a child usually meant having a man around—which hadn't been the situation until very recently.

"Whatever you say."

"Seriously, Dad. The climb alone is enough to wear out a strong person," she said, hoping to get the conversation back on the treehouse and away from her potential maternal role.

"Ah, heck, Jillian, you're a girl! Of course the climb wears you out," he teased.

"Daddy, for that, I'm not going to serve you the apple pie I brought from Hannah's."

"I take it all back," he said with a grin, holding up his hands in surrender. "Bring on the pie."

When Jillian pulled into Brad's driveway on Sunday afternoon, Whizzer and Spot's playful barks competed with the sound of hammering from the backyard. She'd changed into old jeans and a T-shirt after Sunday dinner, hoping to help him finish the monster treehouse that Jeremy would someday use. Brad had already decided to build another one, on a smaller scale and much lower to the ground, in a nearby tree.

He'd said that this treehouse was for adults only—that he had some very fond memories he didn't want to share with his child. Jillian had blushed when he made that remark last evening, just before she'd gone home to her quiet, dark apartment above the store.

And she'd tossed and turned most of the night, wondering what would have happened if he hadn't stopped them yesterday. Wondering if she wanted him to stop the next time.

She sucked in a deep breath as she turned the corner of the house. Sure enough, Brad was in the tree, hands braced on the railing as he smiled down at her.

"You're not going to get finished if you goof off like that," she called up, smiling at his flushed face and big grin.

"I'll have you know I've been working hard," he said, placing his hand over his heart in a theatrical movement, "while you've been goofing off half the day."

"I haven't been goofing off," she defended herself, grasping the steps to climb upwards. She didn't say anything else for a minute, making her way into the treehouse and regaining her breath.

"Do you have oxygen up here?" she finally asked, hands braced on her thighs.

"Very funny."

"You think I'm joking?"

"Of course you are. Now, where have you been all day?" he asked, raising her upright and kissing her quickly on the lips.

"Well, hello to you too," she teased, smiling. "You've gotten a lot of sun." She touched his warm cheek.

"Yes, more than I expected," he said, capturing her hand and placing a kiss on her palm. "Did you go to church like a good girl?"

"Yes, I did," she said primly, pulling her hand away. "I said a prayer for you, too. And I had Sunday dinner with my dad."

"Knowing you, I'd wager the prayer was for me to be more

prepared," he said, taking a step back as if he knew she'd react to his teasing. "How is your dad?"

"He's fine. And actually, I prayed you wouldn't fall out of the treehouse and hurt yourself before I had my wicked way with you."

"Now, that sounds like something you'd get in trouble for if you confessed your secrets."

"Luckily, our church doesn't require confessions."

He walked back up to her, looping his arms around her waist. "You can always confess to me. I'll listen to all your deep, dark secrets. You can whisper your fantasies in my ear any time, day or night," he said softly, his lips brushing her temple.

"Brad . . ."

"I know," he said, pulling back. "We've got work to do. That is why you came over, isn't it?" He looked into her eyes with his blue-gray gaze and she forgot if she'd agreed to help or not.

"I'm ready and willing," she said in a purposeful double-entendre.

Brad laughed. "Okay, then get over here and hold up the supports. I've got to get the roof finished."

They worked for two hours, talking about how Brad was decorating his house, about life in a small town, about any subject that came up. Jillian felt perfectly comfortable, as though they'd never argued . . . or at least if they disagreed, their differences weren't as important as what they had in common. She began to feel very positive about the future.

Only one thought intruded into her perfect picture. Jeremy. She knew she had to bring up the subject now, before he arrived back home from his weekend with his mother. Brad had mentioned earlier that since he'd taken his son to Houston, his ex-wife would bring Jeremy home.

Jillian knew the woman could arrive at any moment. She wasn't sure how she'd react to seeing the wife Brad had chosen, the woman he'd lived with for more than four years, and who had given birth to the son he loved.

"Brad," she said as they placed one of the last roofing boards against the center support, "how is Jeremy going to react to us dating?"

"I don't think that will be any problem. Do you?" he asked, sounding surprised by her question.

"I'm not sure. If you and I spend more time together, away from him, he might resent me."

"We can make sure that doesn't happen, Jillian. There are lots of things we can do together."

"That's true," she said carefully. "And you're right; we should take the dating slow and consider things clearly before we jump into anything that might affect Jeremy. I know he likes me okay right now, but if he's not part of our relationship, he'll feel hurt, and then he won't like me at all."

"I think Jeremy more than 'likes you okay.' I think he's crazy about you." Brad lay his hammer down on the floor. His smile did more to make her feel good about their dating situation than his words. "Don't worry. We're going to have a great time."

"I suppose you're right. I just wondered. I haven't been around children much, except in the store."

"You're a natural," he praised, giving her a hug.

"I suppose I should be more concerned about Greta, Millicent, and Hannah than Jeremy. They seem to have an unusual fascination with our relationship."

Brad smiled. "We're the most interesting thing that's happened in Scottsville for a while, I'll bet."

"That's true. Before you moved back, the most exciting event was two years ago when the Christmas tree in the square blew over, caught a string of lights, and shorted out the security system in the jewelry store. We thought a major crime was taking place right here in Scottsville."

Brad laughed. "I can imagine the sheriff squealing to a halt with red lights and siren flashing."

"That's exactly what happened! He—"

The sound of barking puppies interrupted her recall of the event. Jillian heard the sound of a car engine rev, then stop. She looked at Brad.

"Jeremy?"

"Probably. It's time. I'd better go down and see."

"I think I'll stay up here for a few minutes." She hadn't realized how she'd feel when the time came to meet Brad's ex. Jillian was a little disappointed in herself because she realized she wasn't ready to face the woman. She didn't *want* to meet Jeremy's mother.

"Okay," Brad said, already walking toward the steps. "I shouldn't be long. Come on down if you want. You know you're welcome."

"I know," she answered, but she figured Brad's ex wouldn't feel the same way. Even if the woman didn't want him any longer, she probably wouldn't relish the knowledge that while she had Jeremy, Brad had been cavorting around Scottsville with his old girlfriend.

Still, as Brad quickly descended the tree and jogged toward the sound of Jeremy's voice, Jillian stepped up to the railing and looked at the spot where Brad disappeared around the corner of the house.

Her life had gotten more complicated lately, that was for sure, but as her father had pointed out earlier today, a person couldn't win if they didn't try. And she felt more and more that her relationship with Brad—and with Jeremy—was a prize worth pursuing.

Chapter Nine

Over the next week, sporadic spring showers kept many people indoors. Business was slow at the pet store, so Jillian caught up on her bookkeeping and ordering. As soon as warm weather settled in for good and the end of the school year was in sight, parents would give in to demands for a kitten or puppy. Children would pursue a summer project of raising guppies, or caring for an iguana, or breeding hamsters. She'd better have the right inventory or they'd drive to Tyler to shop.

The rainy, cooler weather didn't keep Brad and Jeremy from running errands each afternoon. They'd come by the store with no pretense of needing puppy supplies. Sometimes Brad would suggest dinner out, other times he'd invite her over to the house for her opinion on arranging furniture or suggesting new purchases. They made a tentative plan to drive back to Gladewater for an antique school desk.

As the weekend approached, Jillian noticed one unanticipated constant in her relationship with Brad: his son. Wherever they ate—whether a quick lunch at Hannah's or a drive to a nearby town for dinner—Jeremy went along. Brad never asked, but rather assumed she'd want the boy with them. And although Jillian grew closer to Jeremy every day, she longed for the time she could share more than a stolen kiss with his father. She and Brad had the most effective moral monitor in existence— a five year old.

Jillian could have kicked herself for being selfish enough to want Brad alone, away from his son. She also knew Jeremy needed time to adjust to his new home and town, so she felt doubly bad for wishing Brad didn't try so hard to include his son in all their activities. But darn it, she wanted Brad alone! She wanted to snuggle with him on her couch, with only Cleo's watchful eyes. She wanted to kiss him freely, letting her hands roam his strong, tempting body, without a little boy asking, "What'cha doin'?"

Brad was a great father, though, she had to admit. He'd enrolled his son in a morning preschool program so he could get his computer programming work done early in the day. He'd told her that if he didn't finish, he waited until Jeremy took his nap. In the fall, Jeremy would start kindergarten, so Brad would have more time.

Jillian looked forward to that momentous event with every fiber of her being. She envisioned closing the store, then walking into the Patterson home to have her wicked way with Brad right there on his desk. The more she thought about the fantasy, the more frustrated she became.

On Saturday afternoon, two weeks from the day they'd almost made love in the treehouse, she reached her saturation point.

Brad arrived at the store, a cheerful bouquet of carnations, daisies, and miniature tiger lilies in his hand. She stood beside the check-out counter, her arms folded loosely across her chest, and admired the way he filled out his tailored shirt. He looked pretty good in his chinos, too. Kind of preppy, but she knew there was a devil lurking somewhere beneath that conservative exterior.

"How pretty," she said, accepting the flowers, smiling up at him. "I have a vase in the back." She headed toward the storeroom, feeling his eyes on her as she listened to his footsteps trail her into the supply room.

Now if he'd just follow up the flowers with a dinner invitation for the two of them. Or, if he didn't, she'd ask him upstairs for a casual supper and maybe a video. They didn't have to do much, as long as they spent some time together.

"Jeremy picked them out," Brad told her as she arranged the stems in the water. "We went to the mall today to get him some short-sleeve shirts and shorts and he saw them at a stand."

"Oh, that's nice," Jillian replied, some of the pleasure fading as she realized these were not a romantic gift from Brad, but a friendly one from a five year old. "Where is Jeremy?"

"With Brenda," Brad said, shoving his hands in his pockets and smiling as though he hadn't a care in the world. Didn't the man realize he was about to get attacked by a sex-crazed pet store owner?

She wiped her hands on a towel, then sauntered over to where Brad leaned one hip against the counter. "I'm about ready to close," she said softly. "Would you like to do something . . . like maybe get some dinner, or come upstairs and watch a video?"

Brad swallowed, his hands still in his pockets. What was wrong with him? The man she'd rolled on the treehouse floor with wouldn't have hesitated to put his arms around her and pull her close. The Brad who had moved back to Scottsville over a month ago craved physical contact like a puppy craved attention. She wasn't sure she knew this version of Brad.

"What's wrong?" she asked, stopping herself from touching him when he obviously didn't return her need for affection.

"Nothing," he said. "It's just that Brenda is going to be here any minute. She's bringing Jeremy by so we can—"

Jillian threw up her hands. "Oh, so you aren't free this evening. I was under the impression that we might have a little time alone for a change." As soon as the words were out, she realized how they sounded. She pinched her nose, a whopper of a headache coming on. "I'm sorry. I shouldn't have said that. You caught me at a bad time."

"Jillian, I thought you cared about Jeremy. I thought we'd had some great times together."

"We have. Every time, I've enjoyed myself. But Brad, that's the problem—every time we're together, we're not alone."

"I have responsibilities—"

"So do I, but that doesn't mean I can't make time for you."

"Jillian, it's not that simple." His expression was so guarded that she couldn't tell anything about his feelings. Where had the old Brad gone? Why was he acting like she was totally off-limits?

"Then tell me what's wrong! Two weeks ago you couldn't keep your hands off me. Now you treat me more like . . . almost like Brenda," she said, so agitated she had to pace the confines of the small room.

"Believe me, I'm not thinking about you as a sister. Far from it!" He ran a hand through his hair.

Jillian stopped pacing and watched his body language, which often told her more than his words. Right now he screamed "frustration" loud and clear.

"Then what? Just because we stopped in the treehouse doesn't—"

"Do you have any idea how difficult it was to stop from making love to you up there, with only the birds and the breeze for company? Do you have any idea how beautiful you looked with the sunlight dancing across your skin, or how much those freckles of yours still turn me on?"

"Brad, I appreciate the compliments, but I'm still confused. What are you saying?"

"I'm saying that I realized that day that we spent more time together, that stopping was just as difficult now—maybe even more so—than when you were sixteen and I was seventeen."

"So you've decided hands-off is the only way?"

"Seemed like it to me! Good grief, Jillian, what do you expect? You said you wanted to take our relationship slower."

"But I didn't want it to grind to a stop!" she exclaimed, pacing again.

"Is that what we've done?"

She raised her hands in confusion again, stopping in front of him. "Oh, Brad, I'm not sure. I just know that I want to be with you. What we've done together these last two weeks has been fun, but the tension . . . Can't you feel it too?"

"God, yes," he said, reaching for her. He brought her against his body with a suddenness that took her breath away. Just as well, since his kiss stole the rest of the oxygen in her body. Her head swam with the passion that exploded between them.

She tilted her head, coming up for air once, then devouring his lips with the same hunger. She wanted him so much that she heard bells . . . tiny, tinkling bells that sent shivers through her body.

Brad broke his mouth away. "We have company," he whispered against her lips.

"What?"

"Brenda and Jeremy just came in."

"Oh." So she hadn't heard imaginary, passion-induced bells, but rather the real kind—the ones over her door.

"I thought you made me hear things," she said, the humor of the situation taking precedence over the now-familiar frustration.

Brad smiled. "I tried my best. I thought *you* made *me* hear bells."

Jillian laughed, still held loosely in Brad's arms.

"Hi, Daddy. Hi, Miss Jillian," Jeremy called out. "Aunt Brenda said you two were naked back here. You're not naked!"

"What?" Brad said, the expression on his face showing as much shock as his tone of voice. "What *are* you talking about? Brenda!"

His sister peeped around the doorway. "I did not say you were *naked.* I said you were probably *necking.* And I didn't expect such little ears to hear me," she said, frowning down at Jeremy.

"My ears aren't little," he stated in an offended voice.

"No, your ears are fine," Jillian said, placing a hand over her mouth to keep from laughing.

"Your aunt Brenda thought you had little ears, but she has a big mouth," Brad said, chastising his twin.

Brenda shrugged. "Was I wrong?"

"That's beside the point!" Brad exclaimed.

"It's okay, Daddy. I don't mind if your not naked."

"Thanks, Jeremy, but you shouldn't worry about things like that."

"I'm not worried. I know grown-ups do stupid things like that."

"Jeremy!"

"Well, I do. My new friend Billy said he saw his mom and dad in the bathtub together and they were both naked."

"Jeremy, that's Billy's parents. That's different," Jillian tried to explain.

The six year old shrugged. "If you and Daddy got married, you could get naked together."

"I think we'd better change the subject," she said, wishing that she could dissolve into a gaseous cloud and seep into the wall. She did not want to pursue this subject with the entire family looking on. The only way the situation could get any worse is if her father, Greta, Millicent, and Hannah suddenly walked into the pet store.

"Good idea," Brad quickly agreed.

Jillian thought she heard Brenda chuckle.

"I'm going to lock up," she said. The idea of her father and friends joining them, talking to the amazingly liberal Jeremy, made her shudder. She could clearly imagine the talk of the town square on Monday morning.

And she still didn't know if Brad got the message about their relationship—taking it slow, but not too slow. Necking, not naked. With an exasperated sigh, she turned the sign to "closed" and hoped at least one of them understood what was going on.

Brad mentally patted himself on the back. Thankfully, he finally seemed to be getting the hang of this dating situation. On Saturday night the three of them had gone out together, since there wasn't any choice. Brenda had to get back home, she'd explained, and Jeremy wanted pizza. Jillian seemed uncomfortable, but Brad believed that was more from Jeremy's "misunderstanding" than the fact he'd been included once again in their plans.

Looking back, Brad realized he'd used Jeremy as a shield

against getting too close to Jillian. If they were alone together, all he could think about was those minutes in the treehouse when they'd almost made love. With Jeremy nearby, at least Brad could keep his mind on the conversation—when he wasn't imagining Jillian with her bra unfastened, freckled, and sun-dappled.

On Sunday she'd spent the day with her father, then stopped by the house with a movie they'd all enjoy. Brad imagined that was her way of saying, "Yes, I like doing things with both of you." Whatever the reason, they'd had a good time snuggling together on the couch and eating popcorn.

On Monday morning while Jeremy was in preschool, Brad stopped by the pet store with a new bouquet of flowers. This time *he'd* picked out the delicate peach roses and tiny yellow blossoms with lacy green leaves. The expression on Jillian's face told him she understood that this gift was from him—from his heart. When he'd explained that the peach reminded him of her skin, the yellow and green, dappled sunlight through the live oak, she'd thrown her arms around his neck and hugged him. The fact that two customers paid more attention to Jillian than to the merchandise didn't seem to bother her at all.

Brad had whispered in her ear that if she wasn't careful, her customers would think they were *naked*. She'd laughed so hard that he had to assure the other ladies Jillian was okay.

This afternoon he'd stop by with a half-pound of pecan-caramel fudge fresh from the Gardner Bakery. Millicent didn't make the confection often, but when she did, the sisters sold out in the same day. He'd taken his laptop computer to the bakery that morning for coffee and cinnamon rolls, thrilling both sisters with what they saw as cutting-edge technology. In truth, the laptop wasn't top-of-the-line any longer since he'd purchased it six months ago. In computer terms, his newest toy was nearly obsolete.

However, he did access the Internet, showing the sisters Web sites that sold bakery goods and fudge. They'd been extremely impressed, pondering the possibility of their own Internet address. Millicent wanted a computer now, but Greta wanted to wait. Brad chuckled at the memory.

He opened the door of the pet store. The bell jingled,

reminding him of Saturday afternoon when he and Jillian had both "heard bells."

"I'll be with you in a moment," she called, her voice muffled.

He followed the sound to the puppy enclosure. She was bent over, her red hair floating around her face as she played with two small balls of fur.

"Cute," he said, folding his arms over his chest, the bakery shop bag dangling from one hand.

Jillian straightened, a smile on her flushed face. "Aren't they? They just arrived this morning."

"Well," he said, taking a step forward, "I was talking about *you*, but I suppose the puppies are okay too."

She pushed her hair back. "Thanks. I like them," she said in a teasing tone. "What's in the bag, Patterson?"

"More tokens of affection from your suitor?"

"Oh," she said, taking a step forward, reaching for the bag. "Which one?"

He pulled her close with one arm, crushing the sack between them. "If you have another man in your life, you'd better tell him to take a hike. You're not going to have the time—or the energy—for anyone else."

She leaned back, looking up at him with a challenging glint in her eyes. "Oh, yeah? Is that a promise?"

"Absolutely," he murmured before lowering his mouth for a heart-pounding kiss. As before, he could swear that he heard bells.

"This is for you," he said, lightly squeezing her hand where she held the rumpled paper bag. Her eyes reflected the dreamy and unfocused look that went so well with her tousled curls. "Enjoy it. I'll see you later."

When he turned around, Hannah, Greta and Millicent stared back.

"Good morning, ladies," he said cheerfully, walking toward the door, ignoring their raised eyebrows and knowing smiles.

He imagined Jillian would get more good-natured advice from some of Scottsville's most enthusiastic matchmakers.

Brad settled into a chair in Brenda's kitchen on Wednesday afternoon while Jeremy played in the backyard on her daughter's swing set. She poured him a cup of coffee and placed it in front of him.

"Thanks. I could use a little caffeine to help me keep up with him," Brad said, nodding toward his energetic son. Jeremy hung from his knees on a cross bar, swinging slightly by an occasional push against the lawn. Brenda's yard was covered with bright green grass, sparsely dotted with yellow dandelions.

"What did you do about the treehouse?" she asked as she poured herself a cup from the fresh pot.

"I explained to him that I needed to build one as practice since I hadn't built anything in years. I told him I wanted him to have a more special one, with a fort at the bottom. He's real excited about getting his own treehouse."

"So," Brenda said, sitting down and taking a sip of her coffee, "are you and Jillian real excited about having *your* own treehouse?"

"Very funny, sis. I never said that was our treehouse."

"You didn't have to. When Jillian and I went to lunch that next week, I couldn't miss the look on her face when she mentioned that she'd helped you build it."

"Blushing, was she?" Brad asked with a smile.

"Like a peach."

"Well, she should. The woman practically attacked me. I had to fight her off."

Brenda laughed. "Sure, I can see that happening."

"Believe what you want," Brad replied in an exaggerated, slightly offended tone. He'd told the truth and his sister didn't believe him. Well, he probably wouldn't have believed he'd say "no" to making love if he hadn't been there himself.

He was after a bigger reward than one roll around the treehouse . . . and well on his way to achieving his goal, if Jillian's reaction this week was a measure of his success.

"You were right on target," he said, taking a sip of coffee. "Jillian has forgiven me for acting more like "Father Knows Best" than "Mad About You.""

Brenda chuckled. "The flowers and candy worked?"

"Absolutely. Of course, I think my brilliant delivery style had a lot to do with her reaction."

"If your ego gets any bigger, we'll have to widen the doorways," Brenda scoffed, giving him one of her disbelieving "sister looks."

"Hey, my ego is fine. If I didn't have a good, healthy one to begin with, you women would send me sobbing into oblivion. Jillian doesn't cut me any slack either."

"Good for her. So, what's next in your game plan?"

"There's an open air classical music concert in Tyler on Saturday night. I thought I'd see if you could keep Jeremy for me. We might be out pretty late."

"Or maybe really early on Sunday?" Brenda said, raising her eyebrow and grinning.

"With any luck at all," Brad confided. He paused, then shook his head. "That's not really true. If one night was all I wanted, I figure we could have gotten to that point pretty quickly. But you know what I'm after; I want to make up for what we lost when I went away years ago."

"I know you're not after a one night stand, but you've got to understand you can't just pick up where you left off. You and Jillian are both different people than you were then."

"I know. Believe me, I realize she's changed. I sure hope I have."

"But this weekend could be a turning point?"

Brad nodded. "I think so. Jillian's taught me that I've got to balance myself. I can't jump fully into any role—computer nerd, dad, lover."

"You're not a nerd," Brenda defended.

"Okay, I'm no Bill Gates," he joked, "but seriously, I have a tendency to focus on one thing at a time. I can't do that with her, or with Jeremy. That's probably the biggest change that I've had to face since the divorce."

"You were doing okay before the divorce. You balanced fatherhood and computer . . . guy."

"Yes, but it's easier with two to share the load, even though Karen was busy with her own career. And we only had a condo. No upkeep, not much housekeeping, since we had a cleaning service. Buying the house has been a whole different experience."

"So you're not enjoying that big old place?"

"No, I love it! I'm just saying there's more responsibility now." He drained his coffee and put the mug on the table.

"Don't tell anyone I said this, but I actually like the decorating. I think that admission alone is enough to get me thrown out of Macho Men Anonymous."

Brenda laughed. "Probably, but I won't tell. I'm just glad you've moved back home."

Brad looked out the back window, at his happy five year old, at the large trees, blue sky, and green landscape. Home. Yes, Scottsville was home. He hadn't realized how much he'd missed the town until he'd returned. Now he couldn't imagine living anywhere else. For the first time, he understood how Jillian felt about putting down roots.

"I'm glad too, Sis," he said, giving her hand a squeeze. He looked at her curious expression. She apparently wasn't used to seeing him so serious.

"Okay," he said, smiling to show he hadn't been invaded by a body snatcher, "so you're on for Saturday night? You'll watch Jeremy?"

"Until whenever you show up, dear brother," she said, smiling in return. "Just make sure you and Jillian have a really good time."

"We will," he reassured his twin. "I'll bring him by around five."

Brenda gathered their empty mugs and pushed away from the table. On the way to the kitchen, she turned back. "Brad?"

"What?"

"You do anything to screw up this weekend and I'll make sure the entire population of Scottsville knows your secret hobby is antique shopping."

He winced at her threat.

"And if Jillian doesn't come back with the look of a truly satisfied woman, I'll include a little story about the time I caught you taking a bubble bath when you were ten."

He feigned a spear to the chest. "I'm bleeding profusely, Sis."

"She's my friend, and I've waited a long time for the two of you to come to your senses," Brenda chastised. She continued into the kitchen, but then paused and looked back, a smile on her face. "If you behave yourself, act like the civilized, intelligent man I know you can be, she's going to be my sister-in-law."

* * *

As Jillian put the finishing touches on her hair Saturday afternoon, she felt the same butterflies in her stomach that she'd experienced when she was a teenager. Getting ready for a big date, a dance, the prom . . . that's how she was reacting to Brad's invitation to dinner and a concert in Tyler.

She'd chosen a casual but flowing dress in light blue cotton with small white and yellow flowers. Because the evenings were cool, she decided to take a sweater. Because she didn't know where they were eating before the concert, she decided an extra pair of shoes would be a good idea. The weather could change in an instant, so she threw an umbrella into the tote bag containing her sweater, shoes, and small make-up bag.

One never knew when one might need to touch up make-up.

Jeez, she thought, looking at the growing bulk of the canvas tote, painted with pictures of happy puppies and kittens, someone might think this was an overnight bag. The idea hadn't crossed her mind . . . at least not in the last few minutes. Any thought of Brad always included the fantasy of them slipping into someplace private, and into something more comfortable.

Like maybe a huge bed with satin sheets. The idea made her sigh with longing. Was he ready? More important, did *he* believe *she* was ready to deepen their commitment? She was. She'd have to let him know in some subtle way—like ripping off his clothes and pinning him to the mattress in a move any high school wrestling coach would applaud.

Despite her nervousness, she smiled at the image of Brad at her mercy. On a whim, she threw a silky nightgown into the tote bag and snapped it shut, smiling with anticipation.

As soon as she saw a blur of red out the windows, though, she sobered, pressing one hand to her stomach. Pushing aside the lacy curtain, she peered below to the slanted parking spaces along the square. Brad's truck stood out like a flamingo in a pen of chickens. After a week of small gifts, flowers, and lots of attention, their "real date" was about to happen.

"You can do this," she murmured to herself as she hurried around the room, picking up the tote bag. Where was her purse? Her shoes? She found one of them beneath the bedside table.

The sense of panic increased as she kneeled down, flipped up the dust ruffle, and found Cleo with her front paw on the loafer. Her fluffy tail switched back and forth in a universal sign of cat disdain.

Brad's booming knock echoed through the apartment.

"I might be back early," she quickly told the feline. "If I'm not, you've got food and water. Just don't get into any trouble, okay?"

Jillian grabbed the shoe and jammed it on her foot, half-hopping through the apartment to the outside door. He'd come up the side steps since she'd closed the store early, and she could see his tall silhouette despite the late afternoon shadows.

"Hi," she said, throwing open the door. "Come on in. I've just got to find my purse."

She plunked the tote bag down on the floor, fixed the turned-in heel on her left shoe, and went in search of the small straw bag with a floppy blue flower.

"Isn't this it?" Brad said.

She turned back to see him pointing at the tote.

"No, that's just . . . things. I brought a sweater in case the temperature dropped, and an umbrella in case it rained . . ."

"You *were* a Girl Scout, weren't you?" he said in an amused tone.

"Just a Brownie," Jillian answered, heading for her dining room table, where she suspected she'd left the purse. "I got kicked out of the troop after that little swimming pool incident."

"Oh, yes. I remember now. I never did figure out how you convinced those girls that all swimming tests were done in the buff."

"They were very gullible," she said, finding the purse beneath today's newspaper and an empty dry cleaning bag. "And they believed that since we'd be camping at the lake after passing our proficiency tests, skinny dipping made perfect sense." She quickly knotted the soft plastic bag so Cleo couldn't get inside, grabbed the purse, and hurried back to Brad.

"Ready!"

He stepped closer. "Really?" He pulled her close, her rapid breathing not slowing down one bit as they touched chest to chest, hip to hip.

Chapter Ten

"Relax," he coaxed. "Tonight is supposed to be fun, not stressful." He placed a quick kiss on her lips.

"Haven't you heard that part of the fun for women is rushing around, getting ready?"

"I didn't know that. You're teaching me a lot about women, you know."

"That's not my intention," she whispered, searching his eyes. The intense expression took her remaining breath away.

"Why?"

"Because then you might apply your knowledge to other women, and I wouldn't like that one bit."

"Jealous?"

"I would be," she said, kissing him briefly, lightly, on his lips.

"Good, because I can't think of you with anyone else without seeing red."

He closed his eyes, then lowered his head and kissed her gently, softly, until she melted into his arms and kissed him back.

"That's better," he said, smiling as he pulled away. "Now you look more relaxed."

"If I get anymore relaxed, I don't think we'll leave the apartment."

"That's not relaxed, sweetheart; that's aroused."

"Oh."

"But you're right. We'd better go. I don't want to rush dinner to get to the concert, and I'm not sure what kind of crowd this event draws."

"I haven't been for years. I took my dad there years ago, when he was still on the mend."

"Why didn't you go back?" Brad asked, walking beside her toward the door.

"We discovered he didn't like classical music," Jillian said, chuckling at the memory of her father's expression as he'd tried to pretend he liked Handel's Water Music. "He's more of a Tammy Wynette-Jerry Jeff Walker kind of music fan."

Brad laughed. "I can see him now."

They chatted as they settled into the truck for the drive to Tyler, then lapsed into pleasant stretches of silence as the miles slipped by. Daylight slipped away in a modest show of color behind patchy, indigo clouds.

They ate at one of the hotels along the "loop" around Tyler, then headed toward the park closer to downtown. Jillian wished she could unhook her seat belt and snuggle close to Brad's side. She wanted to touch him, and feel his strong arm around her. But sitting like that while driving wasn't safe. She settled on letting her eyes feast on him as he drove, then parked the truck. As soon as he turned off the headlights and engine, silence wrapped them in an intimate cocoon.

When he turned to her, he smiled as though he knew what she was thinking. The intimate look didn't upset her; instead, she felt a growing bond that caused a fluttering anticipation.

Hand in hand, they strolled to the park. Lights high overhead illuminated exposed tree roots and reclining concert-goers. Brad had brought a heavy quilt, a thermos of coffee, and a small bag of Greta's spicy cookies. They spread the quilt on the ground to the right of the orchestra, then relaxed side by side. Brad poured them each a cup of fragrant coffee.

"Flavored?" she asked, taking the warm plastic cup between her hands.

"You could say that," Brad said, smiling over the rim.

She took a sip and almost sputtered as she tasted the liquor mixed into the brew. "You naughty boy," she said, taking another sip. "You brought alcoholic spirits into a public park."

"Are you going to turn me in?"

"And risk the police confiscating the evidence? No way."

Brad chuckled. "I only brought enough for one cup. And it's not that strong."

"Good, though."

"I thought you'd like an after dinner treat."

I'd like you as an after dinner treat, she wanted to say, but didn't. She let her eyes caress him where her hands itched to wander. Brad seemed unaware of her steamy thoughts as he concentrated on the sounds of the orchestra preparing for the opening chords.

He turned to her as the music started. "Happy?"

She was surprised by his question, but quickly answered, "Yes." And she was happy. Content, well-fed, in the company of the one man she'd ever loved. With a smile, she leaned toward him and kissed his lips.

"Thanks for a lovely evening so far."

"So far," he said, a devilish glint in his eye.

"You are a naughty boy," she teased.

"So spank me later," he whispered, one eyebrow raised in a challenge.

She couldn't think of one thing to say to that remark, but thankfully, he turned his attention back to the music. Besides, the darkness hid the blush that heated her cheeks.

She did the same, surprised and amused by his easygoing, provocative, teasing mood tonight. This was a new Brad, one she hadn't truly experienced before. Gone was the awkwardness of their first meetings, the playfulness and restraint of treehouse-building, and the tension of "family" dates. Jillian's heart rate increased as she finished the delicious coffee and leaned closer to his warmth. Soon, music swelled around them.

They listened in silence as the first concerto ended and the next one began. Every now and then Brad would turn to look at her, and each time she felt more certain that she'd made the right decision. She wanted him with a woman's passion, not a girl's infatuation. Not that what they'd shared as teens wasn't real, but their relationship hadn't naturally matured. They'd broken off at the most volatile of times, growing into adults separately. But they had been in love once, and they still cared. They still wanted each other.

"There hasn't been any other man," she said softly as the music faded into the darkness and the cheers of the audience swelled.

Brad turned toward her, his expression unreadable in the dim light. "I don't know what to say, Jillian."

"What do you mean?"

He looked away, up into the night sky. "Part of me is thrilled that I'm the only man you've ever made love with. Part of me feels as though I failed you, leaving when you needed me, denying you all those years of happiness.''

She placed her hand on his arm. ''We'll never know what would have happened if you'd stayed in town instead of going away to school. We can't go back and relive that moment when I told you I didn't want to see you again. All we can do now is go forward.''

He turned toward her, his muscles tight beneath his warm skin. He stroked her cheek with his palm, looking deeply into her eyes. ''Are you ready to go forward?'' he asked softly.

''Yes,'' she whispered, leaning into his touch.

''Then let's get out of here.''

Brad drove toward the hotel where they'd had dinner, mainly because he could re-trace his route and wouldn't get lost. Even one wasted minute was unacceptable, and he couldn't focus on anything as mundane as streets and directions. He'd waited forever to hold Jillian in his arms again, to make love with her without stopping. And she was sure now. He felt her confidence and her excitement.

Hell, he was practically shaking. He had to remind himself to breath. And he silently chanted to be calm, drive carefully, get there safely.

As he pulled under the portico, he turned toward Jillian and smiled, mentally congratulating himself on acting so normal. If he gave into his urges, he'd grab her, throw her over his shoulder, and race to the nearest empty room.

''Would you like to go in with me?'' he asked calmly.

''No, that's okay. I'll wait here,'' she said in a cheerful voice.

To most people, Jillian would appear perfectly normal. Brad realized she was trying just as hard as he was to control herself—either her shyness or her anticipation. He couldn't tell which.

''I'll be right back.'' He got out of the truck as he always did, walking at a normal pace while his heart beat faster and faster as he approached the front desk.

Less than five minutes later, he'd parked the truck. He and Jillian entered the side door, hand in hand.

He smiled; she smiled. Then she began to giggle. He started laughing. By the time the elevator arrived, they were behaving more like teenagers than adults.

"Race you to the room," she said as the elevator door slid shut.

"Last one there's a dumb dodo," he challenged, repeating their childhood taunt. The elevator dinged, then the doors slid open.

She elbowed him aside, giggling as she race walked down the carpeted hall. He avoided her flailing arms, bumping into her tote bag as he tried to pass. Just then a mother and daughter exited their room, stopping abruptly when Brad and Jillian raced past.

"Excuse us," he said, breathing hard and trying not to laugh.

He heard the girl say, "Mom, what are they doing?" just as Jillian reached the door to the room.

"I won," she said, her eyes sparkling, her breathing just as heavy as his.

"Yes, but I have the key," he announced.

Jillian grabbed it from his hand. The mother and daughter passed behind them in the hall, watching them with curious, suspicious eyes. Brad burst out laughing. The woman shook her head in disapproval and hurried her child along.

"You are a terrible influence on me, Miss Snow," he leaned over and whispered as she finally opened the door.

"I hope to be an even worse influence on you before the evening is over, Mr. Patterson," she whispered back over her shoulder with a leering grin that made him laugh even harder.

Jillian hadn't planned her big seduction scene to begin as a replay of a romantic comedy skit from the 1930s or 40s. She could clearly envision Clark Gable or Cary Grant as Brad, while she was sure only Lucille Ball could have played her to a tee.

However, when Brad pushed the door shut and flipped the dead-bolt lock, the laughter stopped. Breathing stopped. Hearts fluttered and threatened to stop. But somehow, they came together in the narrow passageway into the room, prompted by a hunger too long denied.

Brad solved the problem of getting them into the room by placing his hands beneath her bottom and lifting her against him, never breaking their kiss. She instinctively looped her arms tightly around his neck, her legs circling his hips. Then he raised her higher, around his waist. She moaned, slanted her lips so she could gulp in much-needed air, and continued to kiss him as they bumped their way toward the bed.

"Oomph," he murmured as they ran into the dresser. He went sideways, coming up against the four-poster bed with a thud to his arm and her thigh.

She raised her head, trying to focus her eyes on the darkened, unfamiliar room. Brad kept on walking, coming up to the side of the bed with a single-mindedness she admired.

"Nice place you have here," Jillian murmured against his neck.

"Thanks. I tried to make sure it has everything we need."

"A bed?"

"Right."

She didn't try to say anything else. As soon as her bottom hit the bed, he kissed her, deeply and thoroughly, lowering her to the mattress. She grabbed his shirt and pulled him down with her until they both sprawled, half on and half off the high, big mattress.

Brad straightened, running his hands from her hips to her waist, past her ribs and to her breasts. He paused there, looking down at her with a hunger in his eyes she hadn't seen in eleven years. Then he caressed her, molding his fingers through the layers of dress and bra, until she wanted to feel his touch with nothing between them but love.

She raised to her elbows, then reached for the buttons on his shirt. He let her undo each one before pulling her to her knees, then lifting the hem of her dress high over her head. She shrugged out of the lightweight material, watching it float to the rug like a forgotten parachute.

Brad looked at her with hungry eyes as she pulled his shirt from the waistband of his slacks, then pushed the fabric down his arms. She couldn't touch him enough, loving the texture of his skin, the feel of his taut muscles and the springy hair on his chest. A wealth of sensations, all hers. She smiled before she looped her arms around his neck once again and moved flush against him.

"We're still wearing too many clothes," he murmured against her neck, his breath teasing her skin, causing goose-bumps to race down her spine.

"You're right. We've got to do something about that."

She reached for his belt; he searched for the catch on her bra. With single-minded determination, the belt and the bra flew to opposite corners of the room at the same time.

"Now you're wearing a lot more than me. No fair," she teased, tasting and kissing her way across his chest, his heart beating hard and fast beneath her swollen lips.

He leaned forward, forcing her back on the bed again. His hands hooked beneath her arms, lifting her fully onto the wide mattress. The soft cover felt cool against her heated skin, but she craved more heat, not less. She reached for Brad, but he turned away, pulling off his shoes and socks, peeling off his slacks with dizzying speed. He took a moment to take his wallet from his pocket, placing it on the nightstand.

Jillian knew why. He'd always carried protection in a secret compartment beside his cash.

She hoped he brought plenty of the little foil packets.

"I'm getting lonesome over here," she said, rolling to her side toward him.

"We can't have that," he said, turning back to her with a confident smile and burning-hot eyes. In a single motion, he peeled off his briefs, giving her only a brief glance at a very grown up, mature Brad before he pressed her against the mattress.

And then she closed her eyes, smiling as his hands moved over her, gasping as his hot breath reached her breast, crying out when he drew her rigid nipple into his mouth.

She tried to rush him. They'd waited so long. She wanted him so badly. But Brad wouldn't be rushed. With a single-mindedness she found both frustrating and highly rewarding, he made love to her, giving her no opportunity to push him into hurrying their union.

Next time, she told herself, gasping as his fingers teased and coaxed. *Next time I'll seduce him.*

When they finally came together, she felt complete for the

first time as a woman. She closed her eyes and sobbed with pleasure, holding him tight, crying out his name when her world tilted and crashed, shattering into brightly colored pieces of heaven.

Only vaguely aware that he pulled them beneath the covers, she curled against him, once again hearing beautiful music float through the dark night as he closed his arms around her.

They should have talked, Brad thought as he watched morning light wiggle into the room under the heavy drapes. Jillian lay curled beside him, her hand resting on his chest, one leg thrown over his. She smelled faintly of perfume or soap—he couldn't tell which—and a lot like a well-loved woman.

The scent urged him to roll toward her, kiss her awake, and make love just one more time before they faced the new day. But she was sleeping so peacefully, and he truly enjoyed the feel of her beside him, warm and trusting.

She trusted him to watch her while she slept, but did she truly believe in a future together? He wanted to think so. That's what they should have talked about sometime before they left the concert, or while they were catching their breath last night before making love again . . . and again.

A memory of their first time together had flashed through his mind as he'd looked down at Jillian last night, her skin pale against the dark bedspread, her red hair spread around her like a glowing halo. In that brief instant, she appeared just as beautiful and innocent as she did eleven years ago.

When he was seventeen and she was sixteen, they'd made love like the fumbling teenagers they were, both inexperienced but determined. Over the next year, they'd gotten pretty good at pleasing each other, using their love and their overabundance of hormones as inspiration. When they'd broken up, he'd tried to find a special magic with another woman, but after a few kisses, he'd realized that what he and Jillian had shared was vastly different. He'd told himself that was because she was his first love. He'd convinced himself that the rush of passion he'd experienced with her was unique because she was his first, and he was hers. As the years went on, he'd pushed the memories of Jillian into the attic of his mind.

When he'd met Karen, they'd shared a desire to succeed. She'd wanted to build her career as an attorney in Houston, and he was beginning his climb up the corporate ladder. Later, he'd decided that self-employment was far more satisfying than creating a product for someone else. His business had been profitable, thanks in part to the booming computer industry and the need for customized software. Their marriage was mutually satisfying, if not a passionate affair. Karen had never complained about wanting magic in her life, and whenever he'd thought about what they were missing, he'd told himself passion wasn't important. He'd packed and re-packed the memory of Jillian beside the lake, in the backseat of his car, in her bedroom when they could manage to outwit her father.

But no woman had ever replaced Jillian in his thoughts, or in his heart. He'd only managed to fool himself into believing he didn't need her magic.

He could have asked her to marry him last night, but he hadn't. He'd figured that question would have caused her green eyes to widen, her muscles to tense, and her long legs to carry her right out of this room . . . and possibly his life. He sensed Jillian wasn't ready to hear his declaration of love, nor was she ready to make such a commitment. She'd been single a long time; perhaps she didn't think she could adapt to life as a wife and stepmother.

Brad had faith in her, though. Jillian would be terrific at whatever she decided to do. After all, she'd taken over her father's care at the age of seventeen. She'd pursued a lawsuit against her father's employer when even he wanted to drop the action. In the end, she'd won the judgment and recouped the money they'd been forced to spend for his lengthy care— money that should have gone to her education at Texas A & M so she could become a veterinarian.

Did she still want to pursue her childhood dream? She didn't talk about going to school, but would she if she had the opportunity? Another subject they should discuss, he thought as she stirred slightly against him.

His thoughts churning, he realized he wasn't going to be able to sleep any longer. Restless energy and an empty stomach urged him to leave Jillian's warmth. He slipped out of bed as gently as possible, placing a pillow in his place. She mumbled something in her sleep, wiggled a bit, and then hugged the pillow and went back to her much-needed rest.

Twenty minutes later, he let himself into the room as quietly as possible. Juggling a tray from the coffee shop downstairs, he made it to the table in front of the window without spilling coffee or juice. Using his free hand, he pushed aside the drape just an inch to see where to place their breakfast. The smell of the fresh brew escaped, curling around him like a siren's song.

Jillian stirred on the bed, rolling to her back, pulling down the sheet when she stretched her leg. In the dim light, Brad could clearly see one rosy breast and a milky-white shoulder. He swallowed. The cups rattled on the tray.

He sat everything down quickly, then debated whether he should drink a cup of coffee first, wake Jillian to share breakfast, or forget eating altogether. In less than a minute, he could be out of his clothes and into bed.

No, they both needed food. Unless Jillian had changed considerably over the last decade, she was an absolute bear coming out of hibernation in the morning—ravenous and grouchy. He walked toward the bed, then sat gently on the edge.

All thoughts of coffee and Danish faded as he looked down at her. Beautiful in sleep, her pink-tinged lips slightly parted, she looked far too appealing for any mortal man. He couldn't see her freckles in the dimness, but he knew his lips could trace a pattern from her shoulder to the tip of her breast by following the tiny dots. And he was just about to do that when she stirred again.

"Is that coffee?" she murmured, her eyes closed.

"Yes, sweetheart."

"Brad, if you bring me a cup, I'll love you forever," she said, still half asleep.

His heart skipped a beat at her casual phrase. She was only half-conscious; he realized she didn't know what she was saying, or how he would react. But still, he wanted to believe that she would love him forever.

He leaned down and kissed her forehead, then pushed a strand of curly red hair away from her cheek with a hand that trembled ever so slightly. "I'll be right back with the coffee."

Jillian smiled, never knowing how his heart swelled with love that had always been, and would always be, only for her.

Chapter Eleven

Any morning-after reservations Jillian experienced were pushed to the back of her mind during the next week. She floated through the days, finding herself smiling for no reason other than the fact she was happy. Millicent and Greta came by and pronounced her absolutely radiant. Hannah winked and chuckled when Jillian blushed at remarks about Brad. And Brenda . . . well, her best friend was nearly beside herself with glee.

"I knew all along," she said as they ate lunch on Friday at Hannah's Cafe. "He moved back to Scottsville for you, and now you're together again."

"He moved back to town to raise Jeremy," Jillian explained, concentrating on her club sandwich to avoid Brenda's single-minded exploration of the deepening relationship.

"Oh, phooey," Brenda said, no doubt picking up words from her six year old. "He could have moved anywhere. The reason he moved back was for you. Don't tell me you two haven't talked about this!"

"Well, of course we've talked."

Brenda sat back in her chair, her lunch temporarily forgotten. "What does that mean? Are you saying that you still don't believe Brad?"

Jillian flexed her neck, suddenly uncomfortable. "I trust Brad, but you've got to admit he's a big teaser. And he's not above a bit of flattery."

"Jillian, this is serious! I know Brad's not joking about how he feels, and saying that he moved back to town because you're here is *not* flattery."

"I didn't exactly say it was," she defended.

"No, but you sound so unsure of him. How can you . . ." Brenda lowered her voice, "how can you get *that* involved and not be sure?"

"I'm sure about how I feel," Jillian said, pushing her potato chips around on her plate. "Isn't that what's important?"

"Yes, that's important, but so is believing him." She paused, causing Jillian to look up from her plate to her friend's unusually serious expression. "If my brother hasn't told you how he feels, I'm going to have to talk to him!"

"Brenda, no. This is something we have to work out. Neither one of us has exactly said that we . . . Well, let's just say that we're not pushing the relationship."

"Phooey," Brenda said again, dismissing Jillian's claims with a wave of her hand. "Why not just come out and say that you're madly in love with each other? What's so hard about that?"

"Brenda, shhh!" Jillian looked around the cafe. Mr. Potter was hard of hearing, so he hadn't overheard, but his lunch companion, Dr. Taylor, glanced away as though he might have been listening. At another table, the owner of Ye Olde Tea Shoppe smiled at Jillian, and across the table, the woman who'd opened the newest antique store whispered something.

My God, they're all going to be talking about me, Jillian thought as she blushed. And beside the fact that she might be a topic of conversation over the weekend, she suddenly arrived at the awkward realization that her best friend was right; she hadn't told Brad how she felt about him. Oh, heck . . . that she was madly, passionately in love with him. And he hadn't told her that he loved her either, despite several occasions when they should have spoken up.

Wednesday night, for example, she'd gone to his house for dinner. After Jeremy went to bed, they'd watched television for a short time, holding hands and talking about their day. She's snuggled close, then he'd kissed her. And before they knew it, they were lying on Brad's new couch, breathing hard. Brad had led her upstairs, checking on Jeremy to make sure the boy was sleeping soundly. Then without words, they'd slipped into Brad's bedroom to make love in his big, comfortable bed. She'd dressed quietly a few hours later and slipped home, happy as a clam.

Never knowing how Brad really felt.

Oh, she thought he loved her. She *assumed* he loved her. But he hadn't said the words, even during those moments of high passion when she had to bite her lip to keep from shouting the words, whispering them, sobbing them.

Darn it, why hadn't they talked?

"Earth to Jillian," Brenda said, waving a hand in front of her face.

"Sorry," she said, shaking her head to clear the questions that raced around like frantic, frightened hamsters. Was that a key? Was she frightened of admitting her feelings, or maybe scared of what he might say? But how could that be, when she assumed he loved her, and she knew she loved him?

"Look, I'm sorry. I probably shouldn't have said anything. It's just that I thought you two would have settled all this. I know you've had a reason to be cautious, but I guessed all that was decided when you . . . well, when you two went to Tyler last weekend."

Jillian shook her head. "We didn't talk about things being settled, Brenda. We just allowed ourselves to let go."

Brenda reached across and squeezed her hand. "I understand. I shouldn't have judged. You know I have a big mouth, and besides, I care about both of you too much."

Jillian smiled. "I know you do, but this is something Brad and I have to work out ourselves, and, I suppose, at our own pace."

"Okay, but if you do want me to talk to him, just let me know," Brenda offered with a conspiratorial smile.

After lunch with Brenda, Jillian realized that as much as she disliked the idea of bringing up the issue, she and Brad needed to talk about what they wanted. The more she thought about it, though, the more she realized that she was truly, sincerely *chicken*.

She rested her chin in her hands, staring out into the darkness as a gentle spring rain beat against the long, narrow windows of her apartment. She'd never suspected she was a scaredy cat. After all, she'd faced down her father's former employer. She'd taken out a loan and opened her own business at the age of twenty-five without a college degree or a background in business. She managed herself and her pet store with an ability that seemed to come naturally.

But she didn't want to say, "Brad, we need to talk."

Jillian sighed as she pushed herself up from her overstuffed couch and paced the length of her darkened living room. She'd read recently that one of the most dreaded phrases men could hear from their significant other was, "Honey, we've got to talk." Jillian usually didn't mind causing Brad a little grief; they'd teased each other all their lives, and besides, making up could be fun. However, something about saying the big "L" word made her shiver in fear. She felt like Cleo during a thunderstorm, hiding under the bed until all threat had passed.

Unfortunately, if she and Brad were going to have a future together, she couldn't hide under the bed. The "threat" wasn't going to pass. She was going to have to either bring up the subject in a logical, rational moment, or she was going to have to blurt it out in a passionate moment and hope he understood.

She stopped, hugging her arms as a chill went through her. What if he didn't understand? What if he ignored her admission, or assumed that she only said the words because of the passion? What then? Did she ask him about it, or say the words again in case he missed the first time? Any scenario she came up seemed extremely unpleasant. Scary.

And what if he didn't want to settle down here forever . . . or with her? Maybe she'd misunderstood his intentions and he didn't want to remarry.

The safest route would be to suggest they talk, even though men seemed to hate the connotation. As she walked into the bathroom to get ready for bed, Jillian wondered when she'd worked up her nerve to broach that subject of happily ever after.

Several times over the weekend Jillian thought about telling Brad that they should talk. However, each time she paused, ready to say the words, something happened, or the timing just seemed wrong, or Brad started talking about his plans for the house. A couple of times, he took silence as an invitation to kiss her. After that, she forgot about talking for several minutes, until they were interrupted. Then they couldn't talk anyway, so she promised herself the next time she'd be more focused.

When Monday rolled around, Jillian mentally kicked herself

for never finding the right time. Although she'd enjoyed the weekend with Brad and Jeremy—and especially Saturday night when the five year old stayed with his aunt—Brad still hadn't said the three magic words, and neither had she. Their unresolved, unspoken feelings lay between them like a St. Bernard in a double bed. *Today,* she told herself as she opened the store Monday morning. *I have to make time for this.* After all, what could be more important than their future?

Three new puppies arrived that afternoon, so she spent much of the day getting them settled into the puppy pen, making sure they understood about where they should sleep, eat, and "use the paper." She ended up playing with them for nearly an hour, enjoying the antics of the fluffy Cocker Spaniel-Poodle mixes that a family in nearby Henderson regularly provided.

Brad called after lunch, asking if she'd like to have dinner in Longview that night with him and Jeremy. He'd been planning on dinner for just the two of them, with Jeremy staying at Brenda's house, he'd explained. However, Brenda's daughter had come down with a stomach flu this afternoon and she didn't want to risk Jeremy getting the same ailment. He'd hoped that Jillian didn't mind making their dinner a threesome.

She automatically said dinner would be fine, but as soon as she'd hung up the phone, she wondered if they'd be able to talk later. After they came home, she decided, she'd sit Brad down on his new couch and tell him they had to discuss something important.

With that firm conviction in mind, Jillian called her summer part-time helper, Cindy Price. The teenager was a senior in high school, very responsible and mature for her years. She'd worked last summer and had said she was available when Jillian needed her during the year as long as she didn't have any big school projects.

Cindy promised to come by around eight o'clock and check on the puppies. They'd only be alone for two hours that way. Jillian knew she could relax and concentrate on having a good time at dinner, and later, on talking to Brad in private.

As soon as she closed up the store, Jillian stepped onto the sidewalk and paused before she got into her car for the short drive to Spindletop Street. She took a deep breath of spring-scented air as she gazed at the tranquil sight of Town Square

Park. The blooming dogwoods and purple plum trees, the sunny daffodils and colorful tulips, should have cheered her. However, she felt tension from the upcoming talk, and she wasn't sure why. She knew how she felt about Brad; she believed he felt the same way about her.

But the future . . . would they be together in his large Victorian house that she'd grown to love? Would she still have the pet store in ten years? Would he tire of working at home? Did he really want more children?

Frowning, she opened her car door and slipped into the familiar feel and smell of the Subaru she'd bought three years ago. She wanted answers, she told herself, but deep inside, she wondered if she wanted the truth, or if she was ready to face the possibility that their lives might radically alter.

As she drove away from the square, she looked at the houses she'd seen all her life, the trees that had been fully grown when she was just a kid. Scottsville hardly changed, but the lives of people did—sometimes in the instant of a blown tire or a carelessly spoken word. She'd lived with uncertainty in the past, but she was older now, more settled. She knew what she liked, and what she didn't. As much as she wanted them to be happy *together,* she needed to be true to herself.

Her life was in Scottsville, but her heart belonged to Brad and now, to Jeremy as well. As she pulled into his driveway, she acknowledged her biggest fear was that neither she nor their home town would be enough for Brad in the future. She'd never felt inadequate before; even as a teenager, she'd blamed Brad for their breakup. She'd never tried to compete with another woman for his affections, nor had she imagined herself competing with anything as insubstantial, yet important, as a lifestyle. But that's what their future might come down to— trusting that he was truly happy back in their hometown, that he truly loved her, and that he hadn't settled on either her or the town because of the divorce or his child.

Love might conquer all, she thought as she opened her car door, but she needed more than vague assertions. She wanted assurances, even though a little voice kept whispering that maybe she'd just have to trust Brad, trust in a future with the happily-ever-after ending she'd wanted all her life.

* * *

Life was great, Brad thought as he changed into slacks and a sweater from his faded jeans and torn sweatshirt. His relationship with Jillian was right on track, progressing nice and slow, but nearing that pivotal point when they both felt comfortable expressing their feelings. If it were just him, he would have told her weeks ago how he felt. But Jillian balked when confronted, ran when cornered, and he'd already learned that pushing her was the wrong approach.

A few times in the last week, he'd thought she was ready. She'd seemed pensive, as if she wanted to say something important. Although they'd been interrupted several times, he assumed she'd get around to expressing herself. He wasn't going to push or prod, even when he had to practically bite his tongue to keep from yelling he loved her when they made love.

Especially right *then,* at the crucial, intense moment. He'd wanted to admit that he loved her, that he'd always loved her. But knowing Jillian, she'd probably assume that was passion talking. He'd have to convince her the words came from his heart, not another part of his anatomy. If she doubted him, he'd get angry, which was the worst thing to do.

So, he thought as he slipped on his shoes, he'd keep on practicing patience. As a matter of fact, his schedule would help. Ever since the phone call this afternoon, he'd been excited about a lot of things—not the least of which was hearing Jillian tell him she loved him. He'd waited eleven years; he could wait a few more days.

The doorbell rang. From the pounding footsteps downstairs, he could tell Jeremy ran toward the front door. No matter how hard Brad tried, he had to admit he was a complete failure at stopping his son from running in the house. "Who is it?" he heard Jeremy call out from behind the locked entry.

As Brad took the last few steps, he heard his son shout, "yeah" and open the door. Jillian stood in the doorway, framed by the colors of sunset. She wore a short-sleeved, lime green sweater and tan slacks that accented her red hair and long legs— two of her best physical qualities, in his unbiased opinion, Brad thought with a smile.

"Hi, Jeremy," she said, bending down for a hug. "How was school today?"

"Great! We learned to make collages. Do you know what a collage is?"

"Sure. We used to do those in school, too."

"They're neat. I cut pictures of worms out of a magazine. Do you want to see the puppies?" Jeremy asked, pulling Jillian down the hallway. "They made a mess on the paper, but only because Daddy was busy," he explained as Jillian trotted past.

Brad smiled. "Hi," he said, amused at her helpless shrug.

"Hi, yourself," she said, her voiced already echoing a Doppler shift as Jeremy steered her into the kitchen.

Brad followed, admiring the sway of her hips, the bounce of her curls. One of the biggest blessings in his life was that Jeremy adored Jillian, and she seemed to feel the same toward his son. For just a moment several weeks ago, he'd thought this would become a problem. She'd complained of spending time with Jeremy, and the brief but painful flashback to Karen entered his mind. His exwife loved Jeremy, Brad supposed, but not with the all consuming love of a parent toward a child. He didn't expect Jillian to feel the same way he did about Jeremy. After all, she hadn't given birth to him, or even seen him until two months ago. But the fact that she enjoyed spending time with the boy eased Brad's fears that she might resent Jeremy, or not want to assume the role of stepmother when the time was right.

She bent over to pet the squirming, grinning puppies as soon as Jeremy opened the back door and let them inside. For a moment, he thought they might knock her over in their enthusiasm. He was just about to step up behind her, steadying her with his hands around her waist. Of course, that would bring him up against her rear, and in the position she was in right now, she'd probably assume he was attacking her.

Or at least giving her a little nudge, he thought, smiling as he willed his mind away from fantasies involving Jillian. *Later,* he told his libido. After Jeremy went to sleep, the adults would have time to play. And play they would, he vowed. He felt as frisky as the puppies.

"You'd better make sure they have fresh water and food,

son," he told Jeremy. "Then we've got to get on the road. I'm pretty hungry."

"Okay, Daddy," Jeremy said, rushing into the laundry room for the bowls.

Brad walked up to Jillian, kissing her lightly on the lips. "How was your day?"

"Also filled with puppies. I got three cockapoos in this morning."

"Three what?" he asked, amused at the term.

"Cocker Spaniels-Poodle mixes," she explained, brushing a piece of lint off his sleeve in a nice, familiar way. "Very cute, fluffy, and not too big. They're a favorite with everyone."

"You're a favorite with me," he said, pulling her close while Jeremy finished up in the other room.

"I'd better be," she said lightly, but he noticed she seemed a little nervous. Probably because of Jeremy, Brad assumed.

"Finished, Daddy."

"Okay, sport. Now you and Miss Jillian wash your hands, and we'll be ready to go."

Both rolled their eyes at him as they headed toward the sink.

Brad had mentioned he had some exciting news, but Jeremy's non-stop chatter and imperfect table manners left little time for adult talk. Brad said they'd have some time together when they got home. To Jillian, his casual use of the word "home" made her think of a home for all of them together, and whether that dream would come true.

Obviously, they'd never get around to living happily-ever-after if one of them didn't admit their feelings. Jillian knew the ball was in her court, but she wasn't sure she was ready to starting playing this game. Heck, she wasn't sure she even understood the rules!

While Brad tucked Jeremy into bed, Jillian put Whizzer and Spot up for the night. She straightened the kitchen just a bit, noticing new touches here and there. A set of kitchen towels they'd bought in Tyler, a tea kettle painted like a cat that Brad insisted "they" must have since Jillian loved animals. She'd brought a plant over for the windowsill above the sink, where it thrived in the southern light.

She leaned closer, looking out at the back yard where their treehouse nestled in the old live oak's protective cradle of limbs. Brad's security lights lit up the area, showing the clean new wood clearly against the black bark. They'd had fun up there; they'd come to an understanding, a turning point in their relationship. Now, weeks later, they'd reached another turning point—or so she hoped.

"What are you looking at?" Brad asked from across the room.

His voice startled her. She hadn't heard him enter the kitchen. "I was looking at the treehouse," she said, still leaning against the sink.

"Fond memories?" he asked, walking up and placing his arms around her waist.

"Umm hmm," she said, closing her eyes and leaning back against his shoulder. "I like the treehouse."

"Then we'll have to go back up there real soon. I can guarantee we'll have more privacy, just in case you'd like to admire my backside again."

Jillian smiled, remembering her remark as he'd stood at the railing. "That might be fun."

"Might be?" he asked, turning her around. "Where's your confidence in my legendary prowess, Miss Snow?"

She laughed softly. "You're being conceited again."

"Are you saying I've disappointed you?" he asked, nuzzling her neck.

"No, I never said that. I was just disputing the fact that your prowess is legendary—as in anyone else knows about it but me." Her smile faded, and she added, "At least, no one in Scottsville."

"You think I'm a legend somewhere else?" he asked in an amused voice.

"I have no idea."

"Aren't you going to ask?" He kissed her below the ear, sending shivers down her spine.

"No," she whispered. "I'm going against character and stopping before I ask any embarrassing questions."

"No, you assume the *answers* will be embarrassing," he said, his tone telling her he was rather surprised by her statement.

She shrugged her shoulders.

Brad turned her in his arms. "What's wrong, Jillian? You seem awfully quiet tonight. You haven't given me any grief all evening."

"Do I always give you grief?"

"No. Occasionally you give me a hickey on my neck, but you don't seem to be in that mood either."

"Maybe I have a lot on my mind," she answered, hoping her cryptic response might open up a topic of conversation. She was having trouble getting around to the big issue.

"Is your dad okay?" Brad asked, concern evident in his tone.

"He's fine."

"The store?"

"Fine. Cindy is checking on the puppies, so they'll be fine."

"Well, why don't we sit down and you can tell me what's bothering you. I've got something to tell you, too."

"Oh, that's right. I'd forgotten."

He led her into the living room, turning on the Tiffany type lamp he'd found in Mineola on one of his shopping trips. The greens and blues of the stained glass shade looked perfect on the antique sideboard, and the light appeared soft and romantic in the large, high-ceiling room.

They settled on the couch. "Go ahead," he encouraged. "Tell me why you're not your usual feisty self. Are you feeling okay?"

"I'm fine, really. I suppose you could just say I'm moody."

"Oh," Brad said, appearing relieved, "one of those female things."

Jillian lightly slapped his shoulder with the heel of her hand. "That's very chauvinistic of you, Brad Patterson. I'm tempted to tell your sister on you."

He smiled. "Now, that's my Jillian," he said.

She smiled in return, warmed by his easy use of the possessive. "You did that on purpose."

"Me? I'm just an ignorant male," he teased.

"Right. And that makes me . . . ?"

"Oh, I'm not getting into that discussion," he said with a laugh. He took her hands. "If you don't have a big issue, then, let me tell you my news."

Chapter Twelve

Jillian almost protested that she *did* have something to say, that they needed to talk. But she'd put off the discussion this long; a few more minutes wouldn't hurt. Maybe she'd be able to bolster her confidence while Brad revealed his news.

"Sure," she said, smiling in an encouraging way. "Go ahead. What's up?"

"I've been talking to a software development group in Houston, founded by a couple of guys I used to work with before I started my own company. They've hooked up with an Internet provider who has a new idea for providing access."

"I don't know too much about the Internet, Brad. I'm still trying to figure out the demon computer in my office."

He chuckled. "I remember it well."

"So what does this mean?"

"I'm not sure, but I have to meet with them. What we're talking about could be big, Jillian."

She heard the sudden animation in his voice, saw the excitement in his eyes, and asked cautiously, "Big as in you're going to be the next Bill Gates?"

Brad chuckled again. "Not that big, but still exciting."

"Well, that's great. I hope this works out." She still didn't understand why he felt compelled to tell her this news, or what exactly was the correct response.

"I need your help," he said out of the blue.

"What kind of help?" she asked cautiously. If he thought she could do anything with a computer, he was going to be disappointed.

"Brenda's daughter has a really nasty flu, so Jeremy can't go to her house. She can take care of the puppies, but not him. I've got to go to Houston to meet with these guys right away. I'm asking for a big favor, I know, but could you please keep Jeremy for me?"

Jillian tilted her head to the side. "I don't have to do anything with a computer?"

Brad laughed. "No, sweetheart. Just a five year old."

"I really need to stay at the store, Brad. Is that a problem for you?"

"No, whatever you'd like to do is fine. He goes to pre-school, so you wouldn't have him much during the day. In the afternoon and at night ... well, I know he's a handful at times, but he likes you, and he'll behave. You have that very authoritative, motherly tone of voice that—"

"A what?" she asked, surprised at his choice of words.

"You know, that 'stop it right now' tone that causes puppies and small children to pay immediate attention to your orders."

"Oh, that." She shifted on the couch. "I was just surprised that you called it 'motherly.' "

"Don't you remember my mother's tone when we were kids? I'd say she had nothing on you."

Jillian smiled even though every mention of motherhood made her a little nervous. She wished she understood why. She'd like to feel excitement over the thought of becoming a mother—even a stepmother. At one time she'd assumed she'd bear Brad's children, but the idea had been a vague one far into the future, after college and vet school. She hadn't imagined having children of her own for a long time, but why would thinking about motherhood cause her unease?

She had no answers. "All I know is that tone of voice works on puppies. I suppose little boys are just an added bonus."

Brad took her hand. "So will you keep Jeremy for me? I'll be gone two nights, but I'll hurry back as soon as possible. I know this is a big imposition because of the store, but he's crazy about you."

"I'll be glad to keep him, Brad. You do realize that I haven't had complete responsibility for a child before, don't you."

"I never thought about whether you had or hadn't. I've seen you with Jeremy, though, and you're a natural. I trust you completely. You're not worried, are you?"

"No," she answered honestly. She wasn't worried about taking care of Brad's son; she was worried about whether she'd be taking care of him permanently, and providing him with any brothers and sisters in the future.

Brad didn't pick up on her vague fears. "Great! I'm leaving in the morning, but I'll take him to preschool on my way out of town. I'll need to get his things to you, though." He frowned. "I haven't had this kind of logistics problem since we did a camping trip when he was three."

"Why don't we get his stuff ready tonight? That way I can take it with me. In the morning, write a note so the school knows I'll be picking him up."

He kissed her cheek. "See, you're great at this. I'll go upstairs and get his clothes. I won't be long."

He hurried from the room, leaving Jillian alone on the couch.

Well, she thought, so much for talking to Brad about their future—about the big "L" word. Once again, her plans had been thwarted, this time by some computer geeks in Houston who were developing something she couldn't possibly understand.

With a sigh, Jillian leaned against the arm of the couch, propped her chin on her hand, and waited to get a bag of clothes for the little boy who would grow more attached to her, and she to him, over the next few days. And she hadn't made one bit of progress with his father.

Brad couldn't remember feeling such excitement over a project since the first big one he'd worked on, years ago. Certain coordination efforts would be tricky, especially since he was no longer in Houston, but with e-mail, file transfers, and overnight service, he was sure they could work out the logistics. The product itself had remarkable potential. He couldn't wait to tell Jillian about his trip.

After dialing her number into his cell phone, he waited impatiently for her to answer. Glancing at his watch, he confirmed that she'd still be at the store, as opposed to upstairs. He wondered if Jeremy was playing with those cockerpoodles, or whatever she'd called the new puppies.

"Pet's Plus," she answered on the third ring.

"Hi, it's Brad."

"Oh, where are you?"

"Nearly to town. Just turning off I-20 now," he answered, slowing down for the ramp. "How's Jeremy?"

"He's fine. We've had a good time."

"Last night sounded like fun." She'd told him how Jeremy had helped her feed all the animals, clean out the cages, and sort the toys onto the right display shelves and bins. The call home had helped relieve the boredom of a generic hotel room after a late dinner with the other developers.

"He's a good helper. I might have to hire him," she said, affection clearly showing in her voice.

"How about dinner? I figure by the time I get to town, you'll be closing."

"Not if the only option is pizza. We ate that last night."

"Oh. Well, I'll make sandwiches. Why don't you come by the house?"

"I've got a better idea. You come over here. I'll take something out of the freezer."

"I owe you for keeping Jeremy. I don't want to make you cook."

"Don't be silly. You've been on the road for hours. Just come over. Besides, I'd like some time with you . . . to talk," she said after a pause that sounded either ominous or inviting. Over the phone, he couldn't tell.

"Okay, I'll be there soon."

"Bye," she said softly. The click of the phone and the subsequent buzzing noise sounded loud and harsh after listening to Jillian's voice.

He disconnected the call, then placed the phone on the seat beside him. He felt good, full of longing to see Jillian and Jeremy, full of hope for a successful new software development. This was his first trip away from Scottsville on business, and the first time to return home.

Yes, home. He liked the sound—and the feel—of that word.

Jillian knew her nervous energy was contagious when Jeremy started chasing Cleo around the small apartment. She resisted the urge to yell, taking a deep breath instead and stating firmly, "Stop that right now!"

The five year old stopped. Cleo didn't, running under the bed.

"Jeremy, you know you're not supposed to run in the house,

and you're especially not supposed to chase Cleo. She's not like a puppy." Jillian gave him her best "schoolteacher" look, fists on her hips.

"I know, Miss Jillian," he said, looking down at his sneakers, "but she looked like she wanted to play."

"Her idea of play is to gently bat a little stuffed toy with a bell, not chase around the sofa and chair," Jillian chastised in a kind, but firm, voice.

"Okay," he said, looking like he'd just lost his best friend. Jeez, this little boy had inherited all of his father's acting ability plus some!

"Besides," she added more cheerfully, "your daddy should be here any minute. I could use some help setting the table."

"Okay," Jeremy said, this time a little brighter. He followed her into the shotgun kitchen, his small fingers trailing along her table top and curio case. She found it amazing that children couldn't look at something without touching it. Sometimes she felt as though she spent half her life cleaning little fingerprints off glass shelves, Plexiglas enclosures, and aquariums.

After handing Jeremy three of everything to set the table, she walked through the dining area to the front window, looking for a familiar big, red pick up. She hoped his business had gone well in Houston. He'd sounded cheerful on the phone. Since she'd already decided they needed to talk tonight—with no excuses—Brad's good mood boded well. If only Jeremy would cooperate, either by watching television, playing his computer game, or something, she and his father could get some long overdue talking done.

Two strong lights pierced the semi-darkness, shining onto the square from the south. As Brad's pick up turned the corner onto the mostly deserted street, her heart began to race. She'd been nervous about talking to him, but the thought of seeing him again after two days caused a different reaction. She'd missed him. After two days apart, she couldn't wait to hold him close, and she wanted to feel his lips on hers, if only for a brief, welcoming kiss.

"Your daddy is parking right now," she announced to Jeremy, who had finished his painstaking placement of knives, forks, spoons, and napkins.

"Yeah!" Jeremy whooped, giving a little jump. Good thing

he'd already put the flatware down! His abundant energy caused her heart palpitations when she thought of all the accidents a child might have.

Just like a mother, her father would say. And Brad seemed to agree. Maybe she was cut out for mothering, but the idea still spooked her.

There was no time to think of the possibilities, though, because Brad's heavy footsteps on the outside stairs sent her and Jeremy to the back door.

"Daddy!" he cried when she opened the door.

"Hey, sport," Brad said, hunkering down and hugging his son close. He looked up, catching her gaze. His smile was enough to defrost their dinner, even without a microwave.

He straightened, his hand on Jeremy's shoulder. "Do I get another hug?" he asked, his eyes sparkling.

"I think I can oblige," she said, smiling as she stepped into his embrace.

"Yeah, hug Miss Jillian, too, Daddy," Jeremy added unnecessarily. "She let me do really neat things, and we had a good time."

"She did, hmm?" Brad said leaning back so he could look at her again. "I suppose that deserves a kiss."

She leaned forward, expecting a quick peck in front of the boy, but Brad lingered, placing his hand behind her head for a more thorough kiss that sent her heart racing.

"Not too much mushy stuff," Jeremy complained.

Brad eased away, his eyes telling her he wanted much more of the "mushy stuff" than a fairly chaste kiss.

"Okay, not too much."

"You have to get married to do more of that stuff," Jeremy explained, taking Brad's hand and pulling him through the kitchen toward the dining room. "Like Aunt Brenda and Uncle Sam."

"Oh," Brad said in an interested, amused tone. "What do they do?"

"Oh, you know, Daddy. They hug and stuff, and kiss when they think I'm not watching. Aunt Brenda told him he gave her belly-flop kisses, but I don't think I was supposed to hear that."

"Probably not," Brad said, hiding his grin behind a hand.

"But that's okay, because they're married. If you and Miss Jillian get married, you can do that kind of stuff too."

"Oh, well, I'll keep that in mind," Brad said, turning his head toward her, his eyes positively sparking with humor and . . . something else.

Jillian knew she was blushing, having a five year old explain married life was enough to cause a four-alarm blaze. But Brad's look caused even more heat.

"Yeah," Jeremy continued, pointing to the table. "See, I set the table. Miss Jillian showed me how to do it proper last night. We had pizza, though, so we didn't need the knife and spoons, except for the ice cream later. I think Miss Jillian would be a great mom, so if you want to get married, it's okay with me."

Jillian blinked, not sure she'd just heard pizza, ice cream, place settings, and marriage in one short burst of energy. But sure enough, that's what he'd said, because Brad was laughing, clapping his son on the back.

"I'm glad you approve, Jeremy, but I think we'll have to talk about that some other time, okay? Right now, Miss Jillian looks like she could use some help in the kitchen."

"Okay," Jeremy said, turning away from the dining room table. "I'll help."

"Why don't you go wash up?" Brad suggested. "I'll help with dinner."

"I just washed my hands!"

"You were playing with Cleo," Jillian reminded him.

"But I didn't touch her!"

"Jeremy," Brad warned.

"Okay," the boy said, slumping his shoulders and heading down the short hall to the bathroom.

Brad turned to her, still grinning. "Kids can say the darnedest things, can't they?" he quipped.

"They certainly can. I don't know where they get these ideas."

"Oh, I think I can imagine," he said, reaching for her waist and pulling her close.

"Not now!" she warned. "He'll be back, and I don't want another scolding about too much mushy stuff. I'm still getting over his first announcement. I'm afraid next time, we'll get a lecture on where babies come from. I'm just not ready for that.''

Brad laughed, letting her go, but following her into the small kitchen. ''Can I help?''

For a moment, she froze, thinking he meant with ''where babies came from.'' But then she realized he was referring to dinner—that meal she was trying to get on the table. She hoped her still-pink cheeks didn't give her thoughts away.

''Sure,'' she said cheerfully. ''Just put this casserole dish on the table. Here's a hot pad to go underneath.''

She handed everything to Brad, then turned toward the sink when she was alone. Fanning her cheeks with a potholder, she wondered why she'd decided they needed to talk tonight, of all nights, and if she'd have the courage to go through with her decision.

Jeremy's energy finally gave out. Brad suggested he sit on Miss Jillian's bed and play with his computer game. When they went in to check on him fifteen minutes later, after coffee to finish off the meal, he'd curled up on his side, game in one hand, Cleo lying against his legs.

She'd apparently forgiven him for chasing her around the living room earlier, Jillian thought, smiling at the picture they presented.

''He's growing up so fast,'' Brad whispered from beside her as they looked at his sleeping son, ''but in some ways, he's still a baby.''

''I've heard Brenda say that they're always your baby,'' Jillian remarked, also watching Jeremy with tenderness. She had grown more attached to him, just as she'd suspected. And he'd obviously been thinking of her relationship with his dad; otherwise, he wouldn't have commented on marriage and ''mushy stuff.''

Brad gazed at his son for another moment, then took Jillian's arm. ''Let's go in the other room. He looks like he'll be sleeping for a while.''

She walked ahead of him down the narrow, short hallway, then headed for the couch. Taking a deep breath, she settled on the thick cushions. The apartment was quiet; Jeremy was sleeping. *No excuses,* she told herself.

"So, your trip was good?" she asked as Brad sat beside her.

"Great," he answered enthusiastically. "Tiring, but good. We had a lot of adrenaline flowing the past two days."

"You worked with the two other men before?"

"Yes, right out of college. We had some good times back then," he said with a chuckle. "Of course, we've all settled down now. The first night, we went out. I can't say we painted the town red, but we got a few good brush strokes in."

The thought of Brad partying in some bar or nightclub, getting ogled by women, made her see green, not red. "So, these guys aren't married?"

"One's single, one's divorced."

"I suppose they're good at what they do, though?"

"Sure. This is a really good project, Jillian. I know these guys, and they wouldn't be so involved if they didn't think this would work. The concept appears simple, but requires lots of interface between the PC and the servers. We'll do a lot of testing, of course."

"Of course," she said, dreading the sound of all that technical lingo. She had no idea what he meant by servers and interfaces. However, she could imagine lots of trips back and forth to Houston, which was no short drive. And since there wasn't an airport around, except a small one in Tyler, Brad's transportation options were limited.

"I'm glad you're back," she said, placing her hand on his arm, hoping they could stop talking about this project—which sounded like something that would take Brad away—and start talking about *them.* "I missed you. Your son is good company, but he's just not you."

Brad smiled. "Thanks again for watching him. I called Brenda, and she said her daughter was fine now. That flu just came at a bad time."

"Brad, really, I didn't mind. He was hardly any trouble— and no more than if he'd been a customer." And she didn't want to talk about Jeremy or Brenda, either, as much as she loved them both.

"I'll have to go back to Houston regularly, once we get the project rolling," Brad continued, obviously having no clue she wasn't on his same wave length. "I wanted to let you know ahead of time. Not that I expect you to watch Jeremy," he added quickly. "I might even take him with me once I know how our work schedules will be. Getting an apartment in the city might even be a good idea, at least for a couple of months. I hate to stay in hotels, and that way, Jeremy could have his own things around."

"I can take care of him," she said, feeling defensive about Jeremy *and* Brad going off to Houston—especially to an apartment. She'd liked being a mother-figure for the past two days, even though his son wasn't her main focus right now. The idea of Brad, alone in a city of millions, with lots of available women, caused a burst of panic. Her fingers clutched his shirt fabric into a wrinkled ball until she willed herself to relax.

"That's sweet of you, but I don't want to impose."

"You're not imposing!" she responded, giving up the battle to relax.

He looked surprised by her remark. "Okay, so it's not an imposition."

"Brad, don't try to placate me by agreeing. I want us to be honest with each other."

"We've always been honest," he said, assuming a defensive tone.

She took a deep breath, telling herself to be calm. "Yes, but we're older now, and life can sometimes get more difficult."

"What's that supposed to mean?" He sounded more agitated by the second.

"I mean that we each came into this relationship with emotional baggage. I blamed you for our breakup. You'd just gotten a divorce . . ."

"My divorce didn't create any emotional baggage," he stated. "If anything, I felt a lot more free."

"Well, okay. You were free, then you moved back here. This isn't a liberating place, Brad. You moved from one set of restrictions to another."

"What are you talking about?" he asked, genuinely amazed.

"I'm talking about how you came back here to raise your son in your hometown, and then got involved with me, and—"

"Wait a minute, Jillian. You've gotten things confused. I moved back here *to get involved* with you again. Our relationship didn't just happen. Do you honestly think I stumbled upon your pet store while visiting my sister?''

"Well, no," she said carefully. "I suppose you knew all along where I was and what I was doing. Brenda probably gave you updates."

"She gave me updates because I *asked*, you dodo," he said, adult frustration warring with his childish self. He ran a hand through his hair. "Look, I'm not sure what this is all about. If you're mad because I'm going to have to be in Houston over the next couple of months, then I'm sorry. But I'm self-employed, Jillian. I have to travel a little. I have to do business with other people at times."

"I'm not mad, and I'm not . . . resentful that you're going to be in Houston," she said fiercely.

"Then what's all this talk about restrictions, involvements and baggage? Have you been reading too many of those self-help articles."

She felt her cheeks start to burn. "Brad Patterson, don't start criticizing me or what I read. You don't know a thing about it!"

"Exactly! And every time I try to get a straight answer, you make another comment that sounds like you're one of those talk show hosts."

"I've tried to talk to you for over a week, but we never have time."

"That sounds like a bunch of bull, Jillian," he accused. "We've had lots of time for other things. Going out to eat, talking about the house, playing with Jeremy . . . even making love."

He was right, but she wasn't about to admit it, so she folded her arms across her chest and pressed her lips together.

"Oh, that looks real grown-up," he said sarcastically.

"I'm not feeling very grownup at the moment."

"I can tell. Does that mean we're through talking for tonight?" He leaned forward as though he was ready to spring off the couch.

"No! There are things we need to discuss."

He settled back against the cushions. "Okay, then talk."

"I said *we* need to talk. I'm not going to talk *at* you."

"Since I have no idea what's on your mind, you're going

to have to start. Otherwise, we'll both get pretty tired of sitting here all night.''

He was in no mood to listen. She was in no mood to tell him how she felt. Heck, at the moment, she wasn't sure *what* she was feeling. Anger, a bit of jealousy, that was certain. But how could she talk about love and happily ever after when they were in the midst of an argument?

She took a deep breath. Then another. Still, the words wouldn't come. Her brain refused to cooperate with her mouth.

"Jillian, just tell me. Whatever it is, just say it.''

"Okay, okay. I'm trying,'' she said, exasperated that this night had gone so wrong, so fast. She took another deep breath. "I wanted to talk to you about where our relationship was headed.''

There, she'd said it. Instead of light bulbs going off over Brad's head, as she'd hoped, he kept looking at her with a confused expression on his face.

"Maybe it's just me. Maybe I'm too tired tonight to understand,'' he said, shaking his head. "But could you please make sense?''

She couldn't do this. Not now. She was in no mood to admit to this man on her couch that she was in love with him. "Never mind, Brad. I guess it wasn't important.''

"What? You said you've been trying to talk to me for over a week! You said you wanted to know where our relationship was headed. Then you say it isn't important?'' He leaped off the couch as if she'd burned him. "Are you saying our relationship isn't important?'' he asked, pacing toward the window.

"No, I'm not saying that,'' she said carefully, deliberately, to his rigid back. "Maybe tonight it's not as important as your trip to Houston, or your plans, or whatever arrangements you'll need to make about Jeremy.''

He turned to face her, his expression hard. "That's ridiculous. Everything I've done for months has been for *us*. You and me, Jillian. Not me and my business, not me and Jeremy.''

"And you don't think I've tried? I didn't want to get involved with you, but I did. I didn't want to care about Jeremy, but I do. This is hard for me, Brad. I keep remembering . . .'' She closed her eyes, tears forming. Her throat burned as she swallowed her pain.

"Jillian," he said, coming to stand in front of her, "what I'm hearing is that you think our relationship is a big mistake."

Chapter Thirteen

"I never said that!"

"You said you keep remembering. Remembering the past, when I walked out on you? Is that what you're saying?"

"Yes!"

"And you're not remembering that you told me you never wanted to see me again, that you didn't want my ring. Are those memories wiped out of your mind?"

"No, but I had my reasons."

"I did too, Jillian, but I was eighteen years old. When are you going to realize we're not teenagers any more?" he asked in a tired, defeated voice.

"I'm trying," she said, looking away, blinking away the moisture that threatened to spill down her hot cheeks. "But when you came back tonight, you were so excited about this new project. So excited about going back to Houston, even taking Jeremy with you."

"I never said I was excited about going to Houston. I said the business trips were necessary."

"Going there might be necessary, but I heard your tone of voice. You had a good time with your old friends. You went out on the town. That's not something Scottsville can offer."

"Jillian, you're imagining this. Yes, I am excited about the project. No, I don't necessarily *want* to go to Houston, but if I do, I'd like to be comfortable. Yes, I miss Jeremy. Hell, I miss you too! But I know you have responsibilities. You can't run off and leave your store anymore than I can ignore my business. Don't you think I learned anything from the time I tried to take you to New Orleans for the weekend?"

She sat up straighter, wanting to believe him, trying to look past her pain and into the truth.

"Jillian," he said, gripping her shoulders and leaning down

so they were eye to eye, "I've done everything I could to make our relationship work. I know I've made mistakes. I let Jeremy come between us because I wanted you so much I couldn't keep my hands off you otherwise. I wasn't always very romantic. I couldn't tell what you wanted at times. But dammit, the point is that I've *tried*."

He stood up, his face tired and drawn, looking older than his years. She blinked, realizing that the tears she'd tried so hard to hold back ran freely down her cheeks.

"You asked where our relationship is going. All I can say is that I thought I knew. Maybe I made another mistake. Maybe I didn't realize that you don't feel the same way about me that I feel about you." He looked away, blinking as though his eyes burned just like hers.

She shook her head, but he didn't notice. He just stood there, looking as though he struggled with himself. She couldn't move, couldn't say anything.

"Jillian, I can't go forward on my own. I thought we'd talked about the past. I thought you'd gotten beyond what happened eleven years ago, but I suppose I was wrong."

"No," she whispered, but he didn't seem to hear.

"If you honestly believe I care more about this project than I do about us, you're wrong. If you think I want to leave Scottsville for Houston, then you don't know a thing about me. I came home to build a future with you, Jillian, but I'm not going to drag you kicking and screaming into my life."

He looked back toward the bedroom. "Into *our* lives," he said, gazing toward the bed where Jeremy slept.

When he turned back, his eyes appeared cold and lifeless. "I thought we could start over, but not if you're going to suspect my motives every time I talk about someone I knew in Houston, every time I need to travel somewhere on business. I can't erase the past, Jillian. I'm not a perfect person now anymore than I was then. I'd hoped I was a little smarter, a little more mature, but . . ." He didn't continue, just shook his head, looking down at the floor.

When he looked up, he ran his hand through his hair again, then faced the bedroom where his son slept. "I'm going to take Jeremy home now. I don't want him to know about us . . . about this," he said.

Brad turned toward her. "When you can let go of the past, call me, okay? I'll be glad to accept the blame for whatever mistakes I've made, but I'll be damned if I can live with your suspicions of what I might do, or your fears that this town isn't where I want to live, or your denial that you're the woman I want to spend the rest of my life with."

"Why couldn't you just tell me?" she whispered, tears streaming down my face. "Why couldn't you have said what I needed to hear?"

"Because," he said, stepping close, brushing away her tears with one finger, "you didn't need to *hear* the words; you need to *believe* them."

As she sat on the couch, her body nearly paralyzed with emotions she couldn't comprehend, she watched Brad walk into her bedroom and scoop his son into his arms. Tears continued to run down her cheeks as he walked back through the room.

He paused, his bloodshot eyes full of sorrow. "I do love you, Jillian," he whispered so softly, she barely heard the words she'd waited all her adult life for him to say. Then he turned and walked toward the back door.

No, she wanted to scream. *Don't tell me you love me and then leave.*

The gentle noise of the latch catching made her jump. With barely a sound, he'd walked out of her life, taking his son . . . taking their future.

With a sob, Jillian slumped to the couch. She'd lied to herself, months ago, weeks ago . . . she couldn't remember.

She'd said she would never cry for Brad Patterson again . . . but she'd lied.

"I didn't agree to come over for an interrogation," Brad warned his sister as he took a seat at her kitchen table.

"I'm not going to interrogate you. I'm just trying to understand how two reasonably intelligent people could completely screw up their lives," she said, easing down across the table from him.

"I've done everything I could to make my life right," he said.

"All I know is that my best friend won't eat, can't sleep,

and has turned into a walking zombie. My brother is miserable, and my nephew doesn't understand why he can't go see Miss Jillian and play with all her pets. I'd say everything is pretty screwed up.''

"Well, when you put it like that . . .'' Brad shifted uncomfortably in the chair, knowing that something *had* to happen. None of them could go on like this. But dammit, he'd put his cards on the table, been perfectly honest, and he believed Jillian had to make the next move. He couldn't push her into letting go of the past anymore than he could prod her into loving him.

"Look, Brad, there's got to be something we can do.''

"I've gone over this again and again, Brenda. I can't imagine what any of us can do except give her time.''

"Nonsense. There's a simple solution to this, but you're both too thickheaded to see it.''

"And that would be . . . ?''

"Both of you need to quit second guessing everything the other one does and just be honest.''

"I was honest,'' Brad defended himself. "I told her I'd made mistakes. I apologized. I admitted I moved back to Scottsville for her.'' He placed his elbows on the table and leaned over the hot coffee, disheartened after the argument two nights ago, lost because he couldn't make this right.

"Did you tell her you love her?''

"Yes,'' he said quickly, staring at the coffee cup.

"That wasn't a very convincing response.''

"Okay, I told her I loved her as I was leaving.''

"But you'd told her before, right?''

"No.'' The timing hadn't been right. He hadn't wanted to rush her, to put pressure on her to say the words in return if she wasn't ready.

"This is the first time you told her you loved her, and then you walked out the door?'' Brenda asked incredulously.

"Look, you'd just have to be there to understand. The situation was definitely a 'I love you, but' kind of scenario.''

"There are no 'buts' with love, you goofus. You either do or you don't. Haven't you learned anything in the last eleven years?'' Brenda said, throwing up her hands, looking totally disgusted with him.

No more disgusted than I feel, Brad felt like saying. Maybe he shouldn't have given Jillian an ultimatum; maybe he should have played along with her insecurities and fear for a while longer, but dammit, he'd been tired. She'd said she wanted to talk, only he hadn't realized that she'd wanted to talk about how rotten their relationship was.

"Apparently I haven't learned enough," he finally said.

Brenda fell silent, apparently commiserating with him. Not having his sister yelling at him or threatening him was an unexpected development. He looked across the table, suddenly realizing how hurt she was by all this.

"I'm sorry, Brenda. I don't know what to do."

She remained silent for so long that he assumed she didn't either. Well, he hadn't expected any answers when he gave in to Brenda's demands he come over. That didn't mean he couldn't pray for some.

"Did she tell you she loved you?" Brenda finally asked.

He shook his head. Her sleepy comment in a Tyler hotel didn't count. The idea that she didn't love him caused an ache so deep he couldn't talk.

Brenda made a rude sound. "She's worse than you."

"She's scared," Brad defended, "and she doesn't believe me."

"I picked up on that earlier, when we had lunch last week. For some reason, she can't accept that you moved back to town for her."

"I know. I told her, but I could tell she didn't believe me." Brad pushed back from the table, hitting the arms of the chair with his palms. "Dammit, how can you prove something like that?"

Brenda shook her head. "I don't know. Maybe you're right; maybe she's just got to believe."

"When I think about her not sleeping, not eating . . . I just don't know if I can wait."

"This is like being a parent, Brad," his sister said, reaching across the table. "Sometimes you have to do what's right, even though it hurts."

"Love shouldn't hurt this much," he said softly, taking Brenda's hand.

* * *

Jillian tried to work up a smile for the two children who'd just bought her last pair of hamsters, but the effort produced, at the most, a pale imitation. The mother took her change, gave Jillian a concerned look, then ushered her happy kids out the door.

The bell tinkled, grating on her nerves with it's cheerful ring. How many times had she looked up to find Brad and Jeremy coming through the door? Whether they came with thinly veiled excuses to see her, or with flowers, or just with a smile, she'd always wanted to see them.

Even when she'd told herself she didn't. Even when she hadn't wanted to forgive Brad for breaking her teenage heart.

She blinked back tears, then headed for the front door. Closing time was almost here; she wouldn't have any more customers today. Might as well close the store so she could go upstairs to . . .

To what? she asked herself. Cry into a bowl of canned soup? Stare at her walls until they seemed to suffocate her? Hug Cleo until the cat protested and sought solitude under the bed? If even her faithful feline couldn't tolerate her depressed mood, Jillian knew she wasn't fit for human companionship.

She'd just turned the sign over when three familiar faces hurried toward the door.

She meant to shake her head, to lock the door before they could come in, but she didn't. For one thing, she didn't have the energy. They'd protest, or simply come back another time. Better to have this out right now.

She opened the door, letting in a burst of wonderfully warm, fragrant spring air.

"Greta, Millicent, Hannah. What can I do for you?"

The three ladies hurried inside, then turned the sign to closed and locked the door. "We need to talk," Hannah announced.

Jillian was so surprised that she stood there with her mouth open, her shoulders slumped, her mind blank.

"Come along, dear," Millicent said, taking her arm. "We're going to fix you a nice cup of tea."

Tea wouldn't fix what ailed her, she wanted to say. Instead, she allowed lavender-haired Millicent to lead her toward the stairs. On the way, Greta flipped off the lights downstairs, and Hannah nearly tripped over Cleo, who was twining around their legs.

"Shoo, cat," Hannah said gruffly. "We have important business."

That didn't bode well, Jillian thought, but again, she made no protest as she walked slowly up the stairs with the three older women. She felt at least ninety years old herself, pulling her legs up the last few steps as Millicent huffed and puffed alongside her.

"I'm sorry. We should have stayed downstairs," Jillian finally said as they stepped from the landing into her living room.

"Nonsense," Greta said, heading toward the kitchen with a small bag bearing the label, "Ye Olde Tea Shoppe."

Hannah followed her. "We've decided you needed some girl talk, Jillian. We're not going to stand aside while you fade away."

"I'm fine," she lied, sitting on the couch. *Just where you sat the other night while your world crashed around you,* she reminded herself.

Millicent settled beside her, smiling as she looked around the apartment.

"Where's your tea kettle, dear?" Greta asked from the kitchen.

Jillian thought of the cute kitty tea kettle at Brad's house, the one he'd insisted they buy because she loved animals so much. *Not as much as I love you,* she should have whispered in his ear. Oh, why hadn't she done that? Why had she waited until it was too late to tell him how she felt?

She swallowed, seeing three pairs of eyes watching her, expecting a simple answer to Greta's question. Jillian managed to whisper, "I don't have one," before bursting into tears.

Millicent hugged her, patting her shoulder, making "shushing" noises as Jillian cried noisily, gulping air, making a mess of her face, her life, her dignity.

"That's okay, dear," Millicent said. "We can make tea without one."

Hannah brought Jillian a box of tissues. "I think it's more than a tea kettle, Millie."

"Ohhhh," the older sister whispered, still patting, still hugging.

Jillian finally got control of her emotions, at least enough to blow her noise and dab the last of the moisture from her eyes. "I'm sorry," she told her guests, who appeared to waver and fade as her eyes tried to focus. Greta hovered in the kitchen doorway, Hannah towered beside the couch, and sweet Millicent sat beside her. "I'm just a little . . . unhappy right now."

"Nonsense," Hannah said sternly, plunking the tissue box down on the end table. "That man broke your heart. You can admit it to us. We completely understand."

Jillian shook her head, then pushed back the limp strands of hair that clung to her damp cheeks. "No, you don't understand. It's not his fault."

"It's always the man's fault," Greta said from the kitchen, her voice muffled as she rattled pans in the bottom cabinet.

"This time, I think it's my fault."

"What happened?" Millicent asked. "You can tell us. We promise not to tell anyone else, don't we?"

"Of course," Hannah agreed. "But we didn't come over to make you talk. We just want you to feel better. If you'd rather not discuss what that man did, just say so."

"He didn't do anything except . . . except tell me the truth," Jillian said, sniffing back the last of her tears.

"Men often see the truth differently than women," Hannah advised. "My own dear departed . . . well, let's just say that the man had only one way of looking at things. Black and white, that's how he saw any problem. Right and wrong. Now, I'm more of a 'shades of gray' kind of person, if you know what I mean."

Millicent nodded, although she appeared a bit confused.

Jillian knew exactly what Hannah was saying, but Brad wasn't like her husband. Oh, he could be single-minded, but he was fair.

"Men don't think about things the same way as women," Greta added from the kitchen.

"But he . . . Brad," she said, swallowing, hurting just to say his name, "really was right. Oh, I'm not saying he didn't make a few mistakes, but what he said . . . was true."

"Then why didn't you agree with him?" Millicent asked, more confused than ever.

Jillian looked at the small, lavender-haired woman as though seeing her for the first time. "Well, I . . . I don't know. I don't think I realized the truth at the time. I was too . . . upset."

Hannah nodded. "That happens. I used to get so mad at my Fred that I'd sooner brain him with a flying pan than tell him he was right. Of course, sooner or later I'd have to get around to admitting it, and then he'd puff up like a rooster."

The widow chuckled, her memories bringing her more joy than pain, Jillian realized. "Then we'd make up, and everything was all right again. My Fred never carried a grudge."

"Brad doesn't either," Jillian said softly, looking down at her hands. She'd shredded a tissue into tiny pieces without even knowing what her hands were doing.

"That's a nice thing in a man," Millicent added. "Our father was good about that, wasn't he, sister?" she called out to Greta.

"One of the good things about him," Greta added, clinking dishes from the kitchen.

"Brad has lots of good qualities," Jillian said.

"Tell us about him," Hannah encouraged.

Greta carefully carried a tray of cups, filled with a fragrant brew.

In the middle of the tray sat the sugar and creamer that had been a wedding gift to Jillian's parents. Her dad had insisted she take it when she moved into the apartment, saying that she could use the china now that she had a place of her own.

His eyes had grown misty as he held the delicate pieces in his callused hands, obviously remembering the woman who had taken such pride in beautiful things, and who had so few to show for their years together. He'd said that he always planned to buy her a whole set of china, but she'd passed away before he could afford the costly gift.

Jillian wondered if he still regretted not owning many luxuries while her mother was alive, or had their years together been enough?

"Are you all right, dear? Greta asked if you'd like sugar in your tea," Millicent said, patting Jillian on the hand.

"I'm sorry. I was just thinking about my mother and dad."

"How is Herman?" Greta asked, handing Jillian a cup of tea.

"He's fine," she answered automatically, her mind racing back to Brad. He'd told her of his regrets about their past, but she always wondered if he had any about his exwife and their marriage.

No, Jillian realized, "wondered" was too mild a word. She'd had *suspicions* that he hadn't told her everything, suspicions that he might still think of his ex, or be tempted by another woman. Why would she think about those things? Had Brad done anything to make her believe he wanted to get back together with Jeremy's mother, or had he flirted, or even spoken of another woman?

"No," she whispered.

"No, what, dear?" Greta asked.

Jillian looked up, startled. "I'm sorry. I must have been thinking out loud."

"That's okay. You have a lot on your mind," Millicent said kindly.

"Yes, I do," Jillian answered, knowing she was onto something. A ripple of excitement coursed through her body. "Excuse me just a moment, please."

Chapter Fourteen

Jillian pushed herself up from the overstuffed couch, feeling less lethargic than she had for two days. She negotiated her way between Hannah's knees and the coffee table, then walked into the bathroom, shut the door gently, and leaned against the solid wood.

Without any evidence, she'd conjured up her fears, making them real, placing them between her and Brad. Why had she done that?

To protect yourself, she answered with such clarity that she felt stunned. She flipped on the overhead light against the dusky evening sunset, then turned to the mirror over the sink. She wanted to face herself, face her fears, in the harsh white light. Brad had said she needed to let go of the past, and at the time, she hadn't realized what that meant.

Her face pale, her eyes red-rimmed and her nose bright pink, she truly looked a mess. But she also noticed other things. Awareness sparkled as she gazed at her reflection. She appeared composed, yet determined. Her chin jutted forward, and she stood a little straighter.

Letting go of the past meant admitting her fears, then deciding whether they were more important than her desires. Letting go meant not expecting pain when all Brad had given her since his return was joy. Their past *had* guided her reactions to him, she realized in the mirror's bright glare.

Lord, she'd made a mess of their relationship.

All wasn't lost, though, she knew as she reached for a washcloth. Using cold water on her red, swollen eyes, she then scrubbed her pale skin until she glowed. Her hair responded to a good, brisk brushing, crackling with static energy, shining gold and red beneath the incandescent lights. Those small efforts washed away two days of misery and a decade of melancholy over her breakup with Brad years ago.

Although she'd gotten on with her life, content with her pet store, family, and friends, she'd never felt complete. Until Brad returned and she overcame her anger at their parting, she'd never been ready to proceed with her life. And now that she'd let go of her suspicions, she knew she had a chance at true happiness.

She truly felt like a new woman.

A knock sounded to the bathroom door. "Are you all right, Jillian?" Hannah asked through the thick wood panel.

"I'm fine," she said. Reaching for the knob, she opened the door to reveal all three women. Greta and Millicent pressed close on either side of Hannah's larger frame, the group squeezed into the narrow doorway. All of them looked at her curiously.

"I'm fine," she repeated, then smiled. As Millicent smiled back, Greta looked at her assessingly, and Hannah narrowed her eyes in judgment. Jillian laughed. "Really. I'm better than fine. I know . . ." she said, barely able to speak through the joy that surged with each heartbeat.

"Know what, dear?" Millicent asked.

"I know what I need to do. I know what I did wrong."

"I thought he did something wrong," her lavender-haired friend said.

"No, no, he was right." Jillian grinned as she gazed at each woman.

"Then it wasn't really his fault?" Millicent asked.

"No," Jillian said, taking her hand. "This time, I over-reacted. I did something stupid, but I can make it right. I'm *going* to make it right."

"Good for you," Greta said.

Hannah nodded. "I think we'd better go, ladies."

"I suppose the tea worked," Millicent said, smiling, giving Jillian's hand a gentle squeeze.

"Yes," Jillian said, laughing. "The tea worked great."

Hannah turned the two older women around. "Let's go. Jillian has things to do."

"All right," she heard Millicent say as they walked down the short hallway, "but I really thought this was all his fault. That's what Bren—"

The silence caused Jillian to pause in front of the mirror, her eyes narrowed with speculation. What had Millicent meant by that last remark, and why had someone obviously stopped her from talking?

Brenda. Yes, this whole scenario reeked of her meddling.

For once, Jillian couldn't have cared less. In fact, she may send her best friend a dozen roses and a box of chocolates— as soon as she'd told Brad the three words she should have said weeks ago.

Of course, as much as Brenda loved meddling, she could prove even more useful. Although by nature Jillian wasn't a scheming person, some events were too important to leave to chance. She planned on being totally honest with Brad, but first, she needed to get him alone.

Brad wasn't sure why Brenda had wanted Jeremy and him to come over for supper. Neither of them were good company.

Jeremy wanted to see Miss Jillian, and so did Brad—not that his wishes meant one damn thing, he reminded himself as he drove home in the darkness. He'd told himself over and over that the next move was up to her. He'd done all he could for now, and only prayed that she'd realize he truly loved her and wanted to build a life right here, not run off for Houston or some other city.

Everything he'd ever needed in life to make him happy was right here in this small town, except that now, the most important element of his happiness was out of reach, separated by fears and suspicions only she could reconcile. With a sigh, he pulled into the driveway, the headlights revealing the garage that had yet to be cleaned out, painted and repaired. He'd get around to that sooner or later. At the moment, he couldn't muster any enthusiasm for improving his home. Not without Jillian at his side, offering suggestions and encouragement, or teasing him unmercifully.

For a short time, they'd had the best of all worlds—childhood antagonists, teenage sweethearts, friends, and lovers.

He cut the engine, turned off the headlights, and exited wearily from the truck. All he wanted was a good night's sleep, free from self-recriminations and restless dreams of what might have been. He knew, however, that these wishes weren't any more likely to come true than his hopes for a quick reconciliation with the woman he'd always loved.

Through the deep darkness of the spring evening, he made his way toward the back door. One of his neighbors must be having a party, judging by the soft sound of music coming from behind the house. The air almost glowed, almost like candlelight. They must be burning those patio torches, he theorized, pausing for just a moment to enjoy the clean, fragrant air, the gentle noise of crickets, and the peacefulness of the quiet neighborhood.

He loved this house, this town. He'd believed that Jillian would be happy here. They'd talked once, as teens, of buying a big house someday, and she'd said she loved the fancy Victorian homes that could only be found along the old streets, nestled between large trees on big city lots.

Thoughts of trees turned his attention to his own, and especially to the huge live oak where he'd built the treehouse—

with Jillian's help. They'd had fun those two days. He looked up, remembering rolling around on the just-built platform with her, laughing and loving . . .

"What the hell . . ." he murmured, looking up at the golden glimmer from high in the tree. Shifting firelight glowed from inside, casting flickering shadows inside the roof. Was the treehouse on fire?

With a burst of speed, he raced to the side of the house. After grabbing the garden hose, he thanked the stars that the nozzle was still attached. At least he'd be able to start spraying after he climbed to the top. He turned the water on full force, then ran for the steps, grabbing for handholds as he scrambled toward the flames.

Jillian reclined on the large pillows, propped against the far side of the treehouse. She sipped from a glass of wine, and sighed into the darkness. Bringing all the trappings of a seduction up into a tree wasn't easy. She'd nearly dropped the pillows twice before realizing that she could throw everything into a plastic bag and drag it up the tree behind her. Fortunately, she still had the house key Brad had given her when she'd kept Jeremy. She'd raided his supply of garbage bags and twine, plus added the bottle of wine and two glasses as an extra touch. Once she'd gotten everything in place, she'd lit the candles, her heart pounding with the notion she wouldn't have enough time to get settled before Brad arrived back home from Brenda's impromptu supper invitation.

Calling Brenda had been a stroke of genius, Jillian thought as she smiled into the darkness. Having Jeremy stay overnight solved everything.

However, the candles were rapidly burning down, the night was growing older, and still no Brad. Her earlier euphoria faded, replaced with tingling nerves and a hard knot of determination in her stomach. If she didn't get Brad into the treehouse tonight to explain her change of heart, she'd try again in the morning. Oh, maybe not with flickering candles and soft pillows, but she'd get her point across. Her earlier hesitation about talking to Brad, or even seducing him, had vanished along with her unfounded fears.

Just as she'd decided that he wasn't coming home tonight—and where else would he be going?—she heard the sound of tires turning onto the old concrete of the driveway. Anticipation leaped to life, setting her nerves on edge, making her hands shake as she placed the wineglass on the floor. With a quick glance over the rail, she confirmed his red truck in the driveway.

What to do now? On hands and knees, she looked around, then remembered the music. Yes, a soft melody would help. She flipped on the CD player, hoping the instrumental love songs didn't sound too hokey. However, her plan was that he'd hear the music and then investigate the glow of candlelight.

Much more effective, she thought, than hanging over the railing, waving and yelling, "Yo, Brad! Up here."

Quickly lying back among the pillows, she artfully arranged the flowing blue skirt with tiny white flowers, then tugged one side of the neckline farther over on her shoulder. Better to reveal a little more skin than too little. She didn't want to appear the stereotypical small-town spinster, but, she reminded herself, this dress *had* worked once before.

Just as she heard him murmur something, she remembered the wineglass. Picking up the delicate stem, she posed again, ready for him to come to her ... her prince in only slightly tarnished armor.

She heard him race around below, then curse and clamor up the tree. She'd never realized Brad could be so clumsy. She'd done better with a whole bag full of "props" earlier in the evening! Her heart beat faster as she heard his heavy breathing grow ever closer. One hand, then another grabbed the rope handholds just above the treehouse floor.

With a grunt of exertion, Brad pulled himself up the last few steps, then pivoted onto the platform.

Jillian screamed, throwing her arms up as he turned wild eyes toward her and aimed the nozzle of a garden hose.

"Jillian?" he asked, his tone incredulous.

She lowered her hands, then stared at him. With legs apart and muscles tensed, he appeared as a mighty avenger, a wild-eyed lunatic, a heroic firefighter. She burst into laughter before she could stop herself.

"What's so funny?" he asked in a hurt tone. She heard the nozzle of the hose hit the floor of the treehouse.

"You," she answered, placing her hand over her mouth to stop her giggles. "You ... I thought I was going to be drenched!"

"You almost were," he said, looking around the treehouse.

She hoped he appreciated her efforts to create a romantic scene. Cinnamon-scented votive candles circled the floor, giving the outdoor room a golden warmth. Beneath the throw pillows, she'd placed a soft blanket. The CD player hid in the corner, producing songs that hinted of everlasting love with piano, flute, and violins.

"I know this should be really obvious, but I want to be sure. Are you here to seduce me?" he asked cautiously.

"Yes," she said, affecting a sweeping wave at her efforts. "Is it working?"

"That depends," he said, taking a step closer before kneeling on the blanket. "What else did you have in mind?"

"More," she whispered, overwhelmed by his presence as he loomed over her in the flickering candlelight.

"What kind of more?"

"A forever kind of more," she said, placing the wineglass on the floor. She reached out to him, needing to touch his warmth.

He took her hand, then tugged until she knelt in front of him. "Jillian, tell me," he whispered. "I need to hear the words."

"I love you," she said softly, looking into his blue-gray eyes, feeling life vibrate from his body to hers.

"Ah, Jillian," he whispered, his words as soft as the look in his eyes before he framed her face with his hands and lowered his lips. His kiss brought tears to her eyes. Tenderness and caring furled around her like the gentle spring breeze. She parted her lips, kissing him back with all the love she'd stored deep inside for eleven long years.

She pulled away as the kiss ended, placing her hands over his and focusing on eyes that reflected the golden glow. "I was afraid to love you again," she said. "Afraid because I loved you too much. I knew that if you left me again, my heart would never mend."

"I'll never leave you again. Whatever you want to do, stay

here or move, run your pet store or go to veterinary school, we'll do it together.''

She reached up and touched his face. ''I'm awfully partial to this town, to this house.'' Glancing around the treehouse, she added, ''and to this special place. But I realized that I was using the town as an excuse to keep from giving you my heart. I don't want to go anywhere, but if we have to, we'll go together.''

''Together,'' he said, leaning closer, ''is all I ever wanted. I thought I knew how much, but I didn't . . . until I touched you again.''

He lowered her to the pillows, stretching over her body until she felt consumed by him. And then slowly, they made love amid the pillows and candles, with crickets chirping below and night birds calling above. With love, the most powerful seduction of all.

Afterward, her head pillowed on his chest, Jillian reached to the side and stroked a strong wood post, smiling into the night. ''Now we'll really have to build Jeremy a new treehouse,'' she said, knowing she'd never be able to share this special place with anyone but Brad.

''I'll get on that right away,'' he answered, smiling down at her. ''Just as soon as we get a few more things settled.''

''Oh? Like what?''

''Like a wedding to plan. Rings to buy. Furniture to move.''

''Is that a proposal, Patterson?'' she asked, tugging on his chest hair.

''Ouch! And no, that's not a proposal; that's a statement of fact.''

''You're awfully conceited,'' she commented.

''No,'' he said, flipping over until he lay on top of her again. ''Just confident.'' And then he kissed her once more, his body proving that indeed, her first love, her last love, had every reason for an abundance of confidence.

AUTHOR'S NOTE

Scottsville is a fictional place, but I hope your "visit" to the town is a pleasant and enjoyable experience. I love to hear from readers. Please write to me at P.O. Box 852125, Richardson, TX 75085-2125, or visit my Web page at http://www.tlt.com/authors/vchancel.htm.